I0671173

RESTLESS BEAUTY

RESTLESS BEAUTY

a novel by

DANIEL HILL ZAFREN

TIME TREASURES

Copyright © 2009 by Daniel Hill Zafren

Published by Time Treasures Books, West Jefferson, North Carolina

ISBN 13: 978-0-9778892-7-3

Printed in the United States of America

The cover is a painting Night Lake Landscape, #05, by Maria
© Maria Art

Cover design by Susan Newman Design, Inc.

Earlier noteworthy books by the author, Daniel Hill Zafren:

In a World We Never Made (2001)
A Door Never Opened (2003)
Shadow Selves (2005)
Network of Death (2006)
Not Lost — Just Not Found (2008)

Still waters run deep.

English proverb

PROLOGUE

THE MYSTERY OF TOMB LAKE

Lakes foster legends. Unrevealed to the eyes, the imagination sees things beneath the surface of the water. The mind can lead to apparitions on or about the water accentuating its unknown perils. The lake can be said to take on a life of its own. The vicissitudes of lakes are then compared to the varying personalities of people.

Tales of lake monsters and other strange sightings are passed on from generation to generation as are other folklore. Quirks of nature, such as the catching of two-headed fish, give further impetus to stories about lakes. Unusual happenings become even more outlandish with exaggerated embellishments and repeated telling. Deep dark waters can neither confirm nor reject such descriptions. The stories become self-perpetuating, and hushed whispers swear to their authenticity. Haunting and harrowing tales hold perpetual fascination for young and old.

A fertile example of the growth and repetition of lake legends is Tomb Lake, a glacial lake perpetually fed by a series of mountain streams, located deep in the Adirondack Mountains in New York State. It is eleven miles long and ranges from three to five miles wide. Rather geologically unique, it has steep slopes on the long sides and a murky depth averaging three hundred feet. Even during the summer months, the water is much too cold for swimming. Squalls and fog come and go without any advance warning.

Despite the apparent depth, jutting rock formations seemingly rise and fall at will and add numerous hazards making navigation extremely

1

treacherous. A host of rock ledges and mounds are located throughout the lake. Countless unexplored crevices could harbor creatures both known and unknown. These natural formations provide additional fodder for crafty story telling.

Pastoral parcels can be found at both ends of the lake, places of distinct natural beauty. The Tonawanda Indians of the Seneca Tribe used both of these fertile sites for their crop growing and hunting places until late into the Nineteenth Century. Canoe travel was the only link between the two spots, and Indian folklore still abounds about the arduous eleven-mile journey that could be undertaken only by the strongest tribal members. It is told that many canoes lay at the bottom of the lake, with Indian corpses and native artifacts settled into many of the crevices. The lake unwittingly became a sacred burial ground along with burials at the pastoral parcels. This too shrouded the lake with a haunting spell. More and more local folks in nearby towns and farms started referring to the lake as a tomb until that name became fixed as a point of reference rather than the long Indian name used earlier. The name became formalized by the State and eventually maps began to show that term for the lake.

During the Depression of the 1930s, a road was built on both of the long sides as a WPA project with the hopeful projection of commercially developing the two ends of the lake. These eleven-mile roads took six trying years to build. Portions of the mountain slopes had to be dynamited just to make room for a narrow bypass on each side. Meeting a vehicle coming the other way was a dangerous encounter since few pull off points existed. The roads were never paved and cascading waters from the slopes after heavy rains and melting snows left their condition rugged and inhospitable.

One of the bizarre stories told and retold about this construction period involved a truck driver, David Wendell. One day in early winter he was making his usual trip to the other end of the lake to pick up rock from the blasting to take to the quarry when a blizzard came up quickly. Apparently, his truck veered onto the lake. Since the lake was already frozen, he may have believed he was still on the road. David and his truck never made it to the destination. There were no eyewitnesses, and it was presumed that the ice gave way under the weight of the truck and the truck and its driver disappeared into the depths of the lake. In the spring, divers and dredging never found either one. The story has it that one day during this arduous search an ear floated to the surface.

The anticipated commercial development never did materialize. After the Second World War, a developer did build a bungalow colony at the east end of the lake. He even paved the roads so there would be easy and scenic passage to the twenty-seven bungalows and recreation hall he had built. It was called *Terra Firma*. Teachers from the State as well as from Canada were targeted for the summer rentals. The first year, sixteen bungalows were occupied. The next year brought a full contingency. However, that was also the summer when three of the men from the colony fishing from the same boat vanished. Their bodies and boat were never found. It put a chilling effect on the community. The three families of the dead men left for home once all hope for recovery was gone. The other families could not quite get back into a full enjoyment of the place. With no returning families the following year, the colony folded and fell into disrepair over the years.

The locals who used to take their boats to the lake to fish near the shore or go there for picnics began to feel uneasy about the place and fewer and fewer people went there. Even the most daring would not venture onto the grounds of *Terra Firma* taking heed of the terrifying images of the ghost fishermen wandering there. The lake portrayed the impression that nobody was welcome. If one breached that edict, suffering and death might ensue. Tomb Lake was called sinister, and all were advised to avoid its evilness. People shuddered at its mention. Tomb Lake was shrouded in mystery, destined to become a geographic relic.............until.............

RESTLESS BEAUTY

ONE

"Make it appealing enough and the baby boomers will buy anything," Harold Lancaster exalted to his brother, Frank, as they stood at the decrepit entrance to *Terra Firma*. He continued proud of his own reasoning, "Present them with water property and they'll snatch it up for recreation, investment, or retirement."

Harold and Frank Lancaster, land developers from Florida, could not fully believe how they had fallen into this bonanza. They had just closed on the purchase of the lake, and the parcels at both ends, negotiating the rights to the roads on both sides of the lake for no additional cost. At the price they paid, it was a steal.

Frank looked at the worn and broken sign dangling down from a frail archway that looked as if it would collapse momentarily. He stammered, "Must have been a real bear back then to have gotten to this place. That's probably why it went bankrupt. Looks like the water tower is in good shape for its age, but we better have someone go over it with a fine toothcomb. Everything else will have to go. The roads need to be totally redone too."

Harold nodded. "Best we start from scratch. Condominiums with a lake view will in effect be a gold mine."

Frank laughed heartily. "Maybe we can tell them they can take it off their taxes as a medical expense."

Harold grinned. "And we'll laugh all the way to the bank. Our backers will eat this up."

"What about shopping? You know they are going to want every

convenience."

"There are a couple of large parcels for sale not too far away. Real cheap too I understand. We probably can get them rezoned for commercial use, entice some adventurous entrepreneurs, and the problem will be history. From what I hear, this area is so depressed it won't take much inducement for anything that promises jobs for the local yokels."

Frank looked serious for a moment. "The name of the lake is a real turnoff."

"Not to worry, dear brother. We'll refer to the lake in our offering as Thumb Lake. From here it sort of looks like a gigantic thumb. Our lawyers can see to it that the name gets changed officially. I even visualize a restaurant on a paddleboat that will go back and forth between the two developments. We'll call it *The Green Thumb*. We'll open it to the public and tourists will swarm here."

"Hal, another stroke of genius."

"We are going to be rich beyond our wildest dreams. I see that as clear as day."

With the roads repaired and repaved, sufficient to hold construction traffic as well as early bird buyers, phase I of *Paradise Gardens* began the following April. Contemplated were fifty-six attached town homes in a crescent shape so that each unit looked out onto the lake. Extensive common areas were planned beyond the units to take advantage of the natural beauty of the place. Walking trails, benches and picnic spots would be added.

Glenda Pruitt saw the offering advertisement for *Paradise Gardens* in the newspaper before her husband did. She called the toll free number right away for the information package offered. She had heard stories from Dwight so many times about the summers he spent as a boy in the Adirondacks at Schroon Lake and how he wished he could live up there when he retired. In fact, he had talked about it so much that his excitement became contagious. Maybe this was the enticing opportunity they longed for.

At fifty-seven, Glenda had scaled the business world to her present position as Vice President in charge of marketing at the consumer products division of a world conglomerate. Dwight, at age sixty-one, was one of the top bankruptcy lawyers in the City. Both worked long and stressful hours, and would be the first ones to admit that they were burned out. They had wanted a family, but as the years flitted by that dream slipped away from their grasp. Even the personal relationship was business oriented. Expenses were specifically tracked, and there was a total lack of spontaneity in their social lives and infrequent lovemaking. After thirty-one years of marriage they had a remarkable balance sheet to show for their union but little else. Even the swank nine-room apartment on Park Avenue that they owned outright offered little else but the shelter and travel convenience to their respective offices. Predictable daily routines were dull. Even though they also owned a parking space in the garage beneath the building, they did not own a car as there was no impulse to go anywhere. They rented the space out to others, another purely business arrangement. Weekends often meant working at home. Visits to relatives or to attend family occasions, as scarce as they were, meant merely a taxi ride. They had traveled extensively around the world, again just a taxi ride to the airport. Even the travel became less stimulating over time. The fat balance sheet did not make up for cold bed sheets.

There was a twinge of excitement when the information packet arrived. After dinner, they viewed the DVD. Lots of construction equipment and activity, and the camera often scanned the lake, the mountains, and the beauty of the landscape just behind the construction. Then they looked at the slick brochure, containing detailed plans for the town homes and describing the many amenities planned. It certainly did look promising, even if just for short getaways during the summers. It could prompt them out of the doldrums. Arranging for long weekends at this stage of their careers would not be a problem. Getting in on the ground floor might also make this a sound investment. The pre-construction prices were not outrageous, particularly from a New York City standard. So, the next day, as agreed, Dwight called Harold Lancaster at the number in the accompanying letter to take advantage of a free weekend at the Skybridge Motel for a tour of the property.

The Skybridge Motel and Diner, on the outskirts of the small town of Bent Tree, keeping the name from an early Indian settlement, was the only place to stay in the area. Not many travelers wandered off main roads to frequent a place that had not much to offer. Abner Kressky owned the motel. His father, who long since had passed away, had started it in 1938, capitalizing then on some of the WPA road workers who did bring their families to the area. He had named it Skybridge because he believed that the mountaintops were in reality a bridge across the sky. His mother was also deceased. His only daughter, Rebecca, now in her late thirties, ran the diner. Abner had often wished she had married but she had turned down the many attempts by the eligible men of the town to get close to her. Pretty and hard working, Abner hoped that he might one day impress on her that life offered her more than grease and smoke. Her mother had run off with a traveling salesman when Becky was four, and Abner refused to even acknowledge that he had a wife at one time. A pronounced scar was left in his heart. He had never taken up with another woman even though some had made it known that they might be interested in his advances. He made the motel and Becky his entire life. With only eleven rooms as part of the entire aging structure, he kept it in good repair and prided himself on all of the landscaping he started and maintained. He and Becky lived in a small house just behind the motel. The motel was rarely more than half occupied, and most of that was from Saturday night type episodes. So, when the Lancaster brothers approached him with the prospects of paying for guests at the motel and meals at the diner, Abner wished it might come true even though he was skeptical. Half wondering why anyone would want to build anything at the evil lake, and half disbelieving that anyone else would buy what was being built, he more than once said to Becky, "I'll believe it when I see it."

Three weeks later the phone rang at the Skybridge Motel. Abner was outside the office trimming a hedge. He was beginning to wonder if the phone was even working since there had been no calls in over a week. Hanging up with a nod of wonder and a sheepish grin, Frank Lancaster had told him that the first guests would be there on Saturday, Mr. and Mrs. Dwight Pruitt.

Abner loped as quickly as his sixty-year old frame would allow him over to the diner. A couple of breakfast stragglers from the town were at the tables, and Rebecca was cleaning the coffee urn.

Abner slammed the door to get her attention. "Guess what, Becky, honey child?"

"You found a four leaf clover," Rebecca answered sensing that something was up. She loved her father dearly, and their closeness meant he could keep no secrets from her.

"Better than that. Maybe there jus' is a pot of gold at the end of the rainbow."

"Have you been drinkin' this early in the mornin'?" Rebecca looked lovingly at her father. If only he had an inkling that she stayed close to the hearth all of these years to alleviate some of the pain he felt from her mother abandoning the family. She immersed herself in hard work, feeling her youthful vibrance fading away with any good looks she may have had. As she approached forty, her time did not come and go, it just never arrived.

Abner drew close, whispering so that others could not hear. "The first suckers are comin' this weekend."

TWO

As their rented car started the ascent to the mountainous country, the Pruitts had their first sense of adventure in a long time. It remained undaunted even as they drove through the small rundown town of Bent Tree. It was tested again as they arrived at the Skybridge Motel. The motel was unlike anything they had been accustomed to, and if it were not for the enthusiasm they sensed about the condominium prospects, they might have turned right around and headed home. To put a positive spin on the scenario, they decided to refer to the place as quaint.

There were no cars parked in front of the units, and the only sign of life was a small stream of smoke coming from a building at the end of the row of rooms marked *Diner*. That building appeared to be leaning and was not a reassuring safety or sanitary sight. At the other end of the row was a small building with an old office sign on it that was a relic in its own right. Glenda did take note of the manicured shrubbery and beautiful flowers that made an attempt to offset the dreariness of the place.

The rugged man with a bristly beard that came out of the office to greet them was tall and well tanned. His flannel shirt fitted tightly over a muscular physique. It was not his distinct appearance that attracted Glenda. It was his deep voice. Surely, there were none like him that she had seen or heard in New York City. His mountain inflection was a further attention getter.

"You folks must be the Pruitts. Welcome to Skybridge. It don't look like much, but it is as genuine as it can get. I am the proprietor of this haven, Abner Kressky, and my daughter Becky runs the diner over yonder

11

and does the meanest fixin's in these parts. One sniff and one taste and you'll be hooked on mountain cookin'. We're mighty glad to have you here. Frank Lancaster will be here bright and early in the mornin' to take you on your tour. Meanwhile, here are the keys to number 4. Make yourselves comfy, and meander over to the diner when you are ready for supper. Becky keeps the place open until eight. It ain't fancy but you won't leave hungry. Even city folk can honker down to that."

Abner turned and walked back towards the office. Glenda stared at his buttocks as the tight jeans hugged them. She felt a spark in the pit of her stomach, not sure why and what it meant.

Abner watched from the window as the Pruitts pulled the car to number 4 and as they got out. They unloaded a suitcase and three small satchels. He had to admit that Mrs. Pruitt was one fine looking lady. He would even call her classy. For certain, she was far from what he had ever encountered. He liked the way she smiled at him, and it painfully reminded him how lonesome he was for a woman's attention.

A few minutes later Glenda entered the office. Her broad smile was met by Abner's grin. He loomed over her five foot two frame, and it took her an instant to find her voice. "Mr. Kressky, I wonder if we might get some extra towels."

"Please call me Abner or Abe, if you like. I have a feeling we are gonna be fast friends." He sure was attracted to her looks, and he could swear he could smell the richness of her being. Her hair was perfectly in place, not like the unkempt hair of the local women.

She edged closer to him. "Sure. Abe it is. Please call me Glenda."

"No problem with the towels. I can bring them over, or you can come with me to the shed in the back to fetch them."

"I'll go with you. We don't want to cause any undue trouble. First, can you tell me what you know about *Paradise Gardens* and Thumb Lake?"

He moved real close to her. It was as if he was intoxicated by her. "I'll leave it to Frank to tell you about the development. The lake is another story."

"Oh."

"Tomb Lake is a story alright."

"Tomb Lake?"

"Yup. That's its real name. The Lancaster boys are tryin' to get it changed but the townies will always call it Tomb Lake."

"Why do they want to change the name?"

"I suppose they think it will scare some folks off."

"Should I be scared?" She wondered if she should have said that, or whether he might have caught on to the double entendre.

Abner missed the subtlety of her question. He knew what he wanted to answer, but he thought he might have said enough already. His newly found meal ticket was at stake here. He did not want to spoil his chances of having a bunch of rich customers frequenting his establishment. "I'll let Frank answer all your questions. If that doesn't satisfy ya, I'll fill in." He wondered if she caught on to his meaning.

Glenda followed him out to the shed. She felt a nervousness that her many business years had taught her to dismiss. Even as a teenager she had not experienced such a strong and instantaneous attraction to a male. Was it just pent-up frustration? Was it the continuing thirst for adventure that this trip had triggered? For a fleeting moment she analyzed her life with Dwight. It was comfortable and predictable. In fact, it was down right dull. There was no fire, no passion. As the years were slipping away, maybe she should grasp one last romantic fling.

As Abner closed the shed door behind them, on impulse he took Glenda in his arms kissing her fervently. She returned the kiss with ardor. An outsider looking in might not be able to determine which one of them was more surprised. Abner had expected a strong rebuff, if not a vicious slap to the face. Glenda was shocked to realize that her will power was nonexistent.

Still locked in a tight embrace, Glenda spoke first. Her voice was weak. "Wow, you country boys sure work fast."

They kissed again before he responded. "I wanted you the minute I saw you. I never had that kinda feeling before. You have some power over men."

"It's news to me. I must be dreaming. I never had such a sensation before either."

"So what do we do about it?"

Still fervently holding on to one another, she took a moment before replying. "Nothing, I suppose, dear man. A mutual attraction that we apparently both wanted to bear some fruit. As much as I might want more, we can't. It is our two worlds that have met, and our two worlds must just be a memory."

His eyes were pleading. "But I want more, much more."

She broke from his embrace her body trembling. Gingerly she picked up the towels. "Forget it even happened, please."

She turned and left and could not possibly have heard his whispered comment, "I doubt I can do that."

Abner sauntered over to the diner. It was empty. Rebecca was in the back preparing the breaded flounder for the Friday night special fish dinner. She paused long enough to blot the perspiration on her forehead on her sleeve and to see an apish look on her father's face. "What now, pop?"

He grinned. "The city folk are here. Count on two more for supper, but you might have to fancy the dishes up a bit."

"Clean dishes and wholesome food is all they're gonna get. What are they like?"

"He's rather ordinary but she is quite a dish."

"Oh! The Kressky delusion. Fancying things we can never have. Pop, we spent too many years plantin' our feet on the ground to wish for the clouds."

"Honey, you can't have the things you don't know are there. Once you come face-to-face with them, there is no stoppin' fate."

"Since when did you become a philosopher? I thought you were just a motel keeper and a gardener."

The grin expanded as he wistfully spoke, "There's always room for expansion."

She stopped her cooking preparation and moved closer to him. "Alright, enough of the riddles. Do you mind tellin' me what is going on?"

"All in good time, lass."

"If I didn't know better, I would think you are drunk."

"Drunk on love."

"You foolish old man. Don't you dare do anythin' to spoil our bonanza."

"That is the last thing I want to do."

"And?"

"And what?"

"C'mon, you are plottin' somethin'. You better let me know what it is so I can talk you out of it."

"Nothin', darlin' daughter. I am innocent, believe me. If, however, you should develop a fetchin' interest in the husband, that would certainly help me out. His name is Dwight, Dwight Pruitt."

She laughed. "Why would a city slicker want to have anythin' to do with the likes of me?"

"Don't sell yourself short. You have a real nice smile and a good figure. Best of all you got a heart of gold, easy to match all the gold he must have in the bank."

"Right. Take off your blinders. I look and smell of the diner. Blah!"

"Just do it for the old geezer, won't ya? Doll yourself up a bit and pour on the charm with the coffee."

Deciphering that he was particularly enjoying this little game, she decided to play along. After all, he did not get a chance to fantasize and she would not dare destroy any momentary flash of glory. "We'll see. I'll try to be the best me possible."

As it turned out, an hour later when the Pruitts entered the diner, Rebecca was instantly attracted to the city slicker. Maybe it was the hour when she had the time to fantasize on her own, with pent-up frustrations leading to see and feel what she had been suppressing. Admitting to herself that Mrs. Pruitt was one classy lady, she could not keep her eyes off the man she was with. He was solidly built, with hair perfectly cut and combed, and he had a bearing that exuded confidence. If all city folk are like that, she sure could learn much from them. No doubt, he was a man in charge of any situation. His glasses added just the right touch of mature intelligence. He could easily fill the role of the Prince Charming she always dreamed of who would carry her away from this stinking life.

As they entered the diner, Dwight Pruitt's first reaction was that it was a dump just as the motel was. One would have to be extremely wary about eating there. Then, the interesting woman behind the counter caught his attention. Accustomed to seeing women primped to the nth degree, this woman exuded a simple wholesomeness that he had not sensed for many years. In an instant, his realization was that it was what he had been missing all along. Her brown hair, streaked with gray, was unkempt and straggly. Yet, it was captivating as it rounded out a picture of a woman who was genuine. A ruddy complexion reflected too many hours in a hot kitchen. A soiled apron could not detract from a slim and beguiling body. It was her eyes that held him spellbound. He smiled at her broadly, and a return smile was its own reward.

The diner was empty, and Glenda was disappointed that Abe was not there. She wore this tight white sweater and tapered black pants to further capture his interest. Rebecca, seeing the prettily adorned Mrs. Pruitt, had a pang of regret that she did not have any fine clothing and that she should have at least changed into something clean and fresh. Her humorous nature, always a saving grace, came to the fore once again. "Ah, you must be our special guests. All of our tables are reserved but I am sure I can squeeze you into one closest to the kitchen. I am Rebecca, Abner's daughter. You can call me Becky if you like, and I am the cook, waitress, dishwasher, cashier, caretaker and advertisin' manager of this popular establishment."

Dwight even liked what he heard. Her voice had a deep resonance that added to her charm, and even the mountain twang in her diction was alluring. He chided her, "That's a big bite for a young woman to chew on. During our stay, I am sure we will see all of your talents surface. We'll try to be little bother."

"You will be easy enough if your taste buds are in the mood for some vegetable soup I have been tendin' to, as well as fried flounder with mashed potatoes, fresh peas, and the peach pie I made this mornin'. If that doesn't capture your fancy, we have no menu here, I can cook you some eggs if the hens back yonder have cooperated. I warn you though, that way there will be no eggs for the mornin'."

"Your food sounds just fine for me," Dwight bellowed as he moved to the table keeping his eyes glued on this Becky woman. It was a feast for his senses.

"It sounds fine for me too," Glenda indicated as she moved behind Dwight to the table. "Is your father around?"

"Oh, he'll be here. He thrives on my cookin' and knows better not to question what I give him."

"And when do the other patrons arrive?"

'There'll be no patrons, but we might get a few grumpy folks but I wouldn't count on it. It's fixin' to rain, and unless there is a special reason they just won't want to fight the mud."

Dwight was further entranced by Rebecca as each moment passed. "More for us to enjoy is the way I look at it. You're a one person army, perhaps even a form of salvation army."

Glenda looked at him. She rarely saw him joke like this or even so animated. His quips were sharp, and she could not remember seeing him in such high spirits. Was it the mountain air? Was it something else? She took a quick look at Rebecca. *This might get interesting.*

RESTLESS BEAUTY

THREE

Frank Lancaster stood before the Pruitt's motel room sharply at 7:00 a.m. He thought to himself just before he knocked, *They've taken the bait. All I have to do is reel them in.*

Inside, Dwight and Glenda were already up, showered and dressed, earlier than they were accustomed to. However, each had an added incentive in facing the day, and it was not the tour of the property. Dwight was totally enchanted by the wholesome Becky. Such natural wholesomeness was a scarcity in urban life. It was an infusion of energy for him. Glenda was entranced by Abe's raw masculinity, a gruff outward demeanor but with what she sensed was a pussycat type internal behavior. The sensation of his kiss had lingered on her lips long into the night.

Rebecca started in the diner earlier than usual. She had slept poorly, thoughts of Dwight intruding on the usual exhaustion suffered from a long day in the kitchen. She conceded that her abject loneliness enhanced his image. Yet, his emergence on the scene while not realistically representing an escape from her physical and emotional bondage, it did have the promise of an exciting interlude from the boredom and drudgery.

Abner picked up on the fact that something was up. He came to the diner at opening time to help Becky with the initiation of breakfast activity, especially with important guests, only to find that everything was already done. She was dressed in a fresh pair of jeans and a fluffy white blouse, and it was unusual to see her in a new apron. While his mind was preoccupied with Glenda, he could not miss the telltale signs of an interest by his daughter in Mr. Pruitt. Was it for his sake or was this for real? He smiled inwardly as either way it would be to his advantage. His first cup of coffee of the day never tasted so rich. The nectar of the Gods.

When the threesome entered the diner, the greetings were warm and robust. Glances lingered and smiles were prompted for little or no reason. Frank and the Pruitts sat at a table. Abner left his seat at the counter and wished them all a fine day. His gaze rarely left Glenda's face, and he felt a warmth spread through his body the likes of which he had not experienced for a long time.

Becky took their order from the choices she offered, noting a special raptured look from Dwight. Her knees were weak, and the cooking and serving aggravated her delight in awakening to her own feelings. Even after they left for the tour of the property, she stood at the closed door until a regular came in for the morning meal. *What to do, or not to do?*

Frank drove the jeep slowly along the lake, pointing out every intriguing feature along the way. A variety of rock formations and vegetation fresh from the evening rain had to be an eyeful for city dwellers. The lake, placid and unusually inviting, glistened in the morning sun. A picture perfect day, and he did his best to portray a scenario the Pruitts would gobble up.

Arriving at the development, they got out of the jeep and walked the property. There were visible signs of construction, such as ground broken, stakes and equipment. There were no workers to be seen, and Frank wondered why they had not shown up for the labor of the day. He made a mental note to call Jack Garland, the construction foreman, when he got back to find out why. Glenda and Dwight were taken by the natural beauty of all they saw, and it did not dawn on either one to wonder why no one was working at the site. After all, it was Saturday, and they did not know that the construction crew was supposed to be on a six-day schedule.

There was a not-so-obvious reason why the construction crew was not at the site. They had shown up early on schedule, especially knowing one of the bosses was coming out this morning with some buyer prospect. However, the first swipe made by one of the diggers unearthed a whole bunch of what seemed to be human bones. As locals, recruited for this building endeavor, and knowing full well the stories of the lake and being highly superstitious, they became spooked immediately. After quickly covering the bones up, they piled into their vehicles and sped away. If Frank had started out thirty minutes earlier with the Pruitts, they would have been impeded to get to the construction area by the caravan going the other way. Even Jack Garland, usually hardened and oblivious to peripheral setbacks, had an eerie feeling. He was not a local, and as the foreman specially hired by the Lancaster boys, he tried to persuade the workers to stay. The fear in their eyes swept him up in the fervor. Once the workers left, he found himself alone. The lake had cast a spell and he had felt uneasy since his initial arrival. Trepidation infringes on rational thought. When one is wary of a situation for a long period of time, and an occurrence appears to validate that wariness, any reasonable explanation blows away as a leaf in the wind. Lore becomes a kind of law. So, even for him he could not stay there alone, and he headed back to his wife in the small house they were renting on the edge of town.

For the Pruitts, the surge of newly awakened emotions coupled with near realization of a dream that this beautiful place represented, and they were leaning towards being the first buyers into this paradise. Frank, a natural salesman, said all they wanted to hear. He pushed all of the right buttons, emphasizing repeatedly that as the first to buy they would have the prime pick of a sky chalet and at a special early bird discount.

It was late afternoon by the time they returned to the motel, tired and hungry. Frank left them to freshen up at their room while he sorted out the papers for them to sign. He knew they would want to study these papers at least overnight, but he had no intention of the weekend slipping away without them signing on the dotted line. He did not anticipate any difficulties, and even his telephone conversation with Jack Garland about the gruesome discovery at the site did not register any complications from his perspective. He urged Jack to call each of the workers to reassure them that there was really nothing about this incident to mar the project. He told Jack to make up some story about the Indians long ago using animals for food and burying the bones to placate the spirits. This would be followed up by the ultimate threat. If they did not return to work, a replacement construction crew from the city would be in place within a few days.

Abner watched the return of the Pruitts from the office, his heart racing at the sight of Glenda in the tight khaki pants and form-fitting shirt. He hoped perhaps more than he should that she would come to the office under some pretense. It was as if his life had suddenly taken a different turn and form. The focus of his thoughts had shifted. From a posture of distant commitment he now realized how truly lonely he had been. Glenda ignited a spark in his soul. Whatever remaining years he had left, companionship and loving affection, as well as passion, had to be a distinct part of it.

Looking up from his reverie, he saw Glenda standing in the doorway looking at him. He had not heard her soft knock or the door slowly being opened. A broad smile crossed her lips. He rose quickly from the desk chair, ignoring any pain his joints had endured in recent years. She closed the door and they embraced, followed by a warm and tasty kiss. Any moment of gentle affection is one to cherish. It is a fragment of gold to store in a personal treasure chest.

When their lips parted, their bodies remained tightly pressed together. There was no need for words. Longing eyes and bodily contact spoke a special language. Clutching at this moment, it would have to sustain them for an indeterminable amount of time. A taste of love, however, can linger for a long time.

Dwight, acting without restraint, was on a similar quest. He just had to see Becky, talk to her, even if he had to suppress any overt actions. He found her toiling over a pot of beef stew that was to be the nightly special. Her apron was soiled and wrinkled, strands of her hair hung down haphazardly, and perspiration rolled down her face. In his eyes, she could not be more fetching. Here was a true slice of natural beauty.

She saw him enter the diner, and she turned off the stove. She wiped her face on the apron. She wanted to give this man her full attention.

He approached, smiled, and said softly, "You look wonderful. I am glad you are alone. I want to talk with you."

She moved close to him. "I am sure I do not look so wonderful. I don't get many men who wish to talk to me."

"A gem in the rough deserves special notice and attention."

"Mighty sweet words. Keep talkin' like that and I'll fall in love with you."

"Now that is a real good idea. I am already quite taken by you. I felt a lightning bolt go through my heart when I saw you."

She leaned closer towards him. "Do you believe in love at first sight?"

"Not before yesterday. Now, I am a true believer."

"What is your wife goin' to think?"

"I think she is quite taken by your father. We have a professional relationship with caring attributes, but the reality is that we have never been in love. I see right now that it is something we have both been missing." He reached out and clasped her hand, still sticky and damp from her cooking chore.

Rebecca glanced downward, a hesitant shyness prevailing in the action. Her words were delayed and fragmented. "This has been my whole life. Any love I might have wanted has been left to dreams. Am I dreamin' now?"

He moved very close to her and kissed her fully on her trembling lips. The dampness above her upper lip filtered down to seal the kiss. Her breath shortened, and there was a thrill, so long lying dormant, racing through her body. It confirmed, as if she really had any doubt about it, that she was very much alive. She meant it as a thought to herself, but it was uttered out loud. "What am I goin' to do?"

"We'll think of something."

FOUR

Back in the city, Dwight and Glenda studied the papers for the condominium. Being the careful and precise business people they are, they did not want to rush into signing them just on mere impulse. They would mull it over, and then let their attorney take a final look. The impetus to go ahead was probably prompted more from Abner and Rebecca than by the real estate promise. They did not talk about the turn of events in their lives, but they had been together for so long that they knew that some emotional outsourcing was brewing. An objective analysis might well conclude that this was inevitable.

Abner could not get Glenda's image out of his mind. A certain upheaval had occurred in his life, and the problem loomed larger than merely how to handle a romantic involvement with a married woman. Did he owe her some honest guidance about the property? He knew all too well the background, the dangers and the manipulating by the Lancaster boys. He would not let anybody he knew stumble into what promised to be a disappointing venture. How could he let a woman he now thought he was in love with get involved in this uncertain endeavor? Yet, if he warned her he would probably never see her again. And, as Becky so rightfully pointed out, it would jeopardize any future motel business with financial prospects.

The construction crew was spooked from the bones discovery, and even the ones that had not yet quit would probably do a rushed and half-hearted job. Compounding the problem was an inordinate delay in the construction work caused by malfunctioning machinery and late and inadequate delivery of building supplies. The Lancaster brothers were reluctant to bring workers up from the city as that would cut into their profits considerably. They would have to pay such workers more per hour as well as provide housing and food for them. They had to ponder other alternatives.

If the Pruitts knew of the incident that was about to happen at the construction site, they would undoubtedly have grave misgivings about proceeding with the venture. It was nearly noon. The weather was pleasant, and a gentle breeze wafted over the work area. The bulk of the crew had returned to work with Jack's pleading, and they were about to break for lunch. All eyes suddenly shifted to the lake. From a placid, nearly glass-like surface, all at once a loud explosion type noise caused deep furrows to take shape as fast moving ripples streaked across the center surface of the lake in the direction of the site. Moments later the ground beneath their feet trembled violently, so strongly that the water tower crashed to the ground. Within seconds it was over, the lake surface calmed and the ground was still. No one was hurt by the fall of the tower. The effect was chaotic on the men. These were ominous signs, and a hushed fear spread quickly among the crew. Whispers questioned what had happened and why they should hang around to see what other fearful event might occur. Later, the Geological Survey would confirm that there had been no seismic activity in the area. In fact, there had never been any record of earthquake activity in the immediate region or even the potential for such an upheaval.

"So, we'll drill a community well," Harold Lancaster said to Jack. "That water tower probably raised more concerns than we could adequately have addressed. You just get the crew back. Get replacements locally if you can. I am sure there is a logical and scientific explanation for this tremor. It probably gets all blown up in the telling of it."

"No," Jack pleaded. "I was there. The bones were bad enough. I am not a superstitious man but there are enough bad vibes here that tell me the project is jinxed."

"Nonsense, Jack. You and the men are just on edge. We just need to despook them so to speak. Our future depends on this being pulled off.

Don't let some foolish, freakish happenings jeopardize this."

Jack knew his explanations were falling on deaf ears. Unless one was there, unless one felt the fear the tremor evoked, it was a tough chore to fully explain the effect on the men. His failure to hold together the splintering work force just reflected a poor management on his part, and he half-expected, half-hoped that he would be fired. Jobs were hard to come by, but sleepless nights and constant worry and aggravation certainly outweighed the rewards. He would, if he could, ride this out as a matter of pride. Like a dark cloud hanging over him, he had a premonition that the future was beyond his control.

To placate Jack and soothe the tension at the work site, the Lancaster brothers decided they needed to do something drastic. They knew that whatever natural occurrence took place, the disproportionate worker response was borne from a fear-panic syndrome. Any wild theory expounded had taken hold, had become exaggerated, and the upheaval was interpreted as confirming the non-fact. While there was no apparent rationale, an irrational action was probably necessary. It was decided to seek an expert in paranormal happenings who would hopefully fully explain the chain of events and use whatever means might be available in the eyes of the workers to rid the place of such sinister developments. The brothers looked on such purported expertise as pure hokum, but they would just have to chalk up whatever expense was involved as a protective measure for existing and future investments in the project.

Making such a decision was easy compared to finding just the right person to effectuate a correction of the situation. There were many crackpots out there claiming outlandish powers of insight and remedial talent. The last thing they wanted was to complicate and exacerbate the problem. Finally, they were led through a series of inquiries and referrals to a philosophy professor at the State University who specializes in explaining the unexplainable. That would be a perfect resolution. Having just the right background and credentials would lend credence to what they knew would be a common sense description of what was and what might happen again.

27

It might be the only kind of sell that the men would accept.

Just contacting Professor Christine Longfellow proved to be a formidable task. Bureaucratic channels at the University, probably as built-in safeguards protecting the faculty, were difficult and time consuming to satisfy. Then, there was the professor's busy schedule. He had to wait three weeks to get an appointment, three precious weeks of good construction weather lost. Even having their attorney call did not lessen the wait period.

So, while the project lay in limbo for the three-week period, and when the appointed day and time arrived, Frank Lancaster still had to wait until into the afternoon at Professor Longfellow's office before he was allowed to enter her domain.

He was taken aback a bit when he saw her. He had expected to be greeted by a much older person, commensurate with the long list of writings and project undertakings itemized in her resume. She was not only youthful in appearance but also attractive, and quite at odds with predetermined professorial looks. The one thing Frank was ready to admit about himself was that he always had a whole bunch of preconceived notions about what people would do, what they should look like, and what weakness they might have that he could exploit. Even finding out that more often than not these preliminary expectations were off the mark, he still let biases dictate impressions and actions. He may not be a perfect person but he sure was a classic businessman. The profit incentive does not necessarily make one a prophet. It might, however, make one pathetic.

"So, Mr. Lancaster, what urgency brings you to my doorstep?" Professor Longfellow stared at him earnestly. He sure was nondescript, and she fervently hoped she was not wasting her time speaking with him.

"Do you want the long version or the short one?"

The professor smiled coyly. "Spare us both. The short version will be adequate."

Frank rethought his proposal and grimaced realizing that this lady was going to be a tough sell and that it might cost more to bring her on board than originally estimated even if she agreed to do it. "The short

28

version may not be as enticing."

"I'll be the judge of that." She stared at her calendar, realizing that this day as every day was filled with so many agonizing moments dedicated to others and that there was always little precious time for her.

"Alright, here goes nothing. Ever hear of Thumb Lake?"

"No."

"Ever hear of Tomb Lake?"

"No."

"Ever hear of what my construction crew thinks is a haunted lake?"

"Lakes are not haunted. The minds of people turn what they see and hear into hauntings."

"Just what I wanted to hear. My brother and I have this construction project by Thumb Lake, formerly known as Tomb Lake, and it is a proposed recreation and retirement community. The crew won't continue working until we show them that the place is not haunted."

"Where is this lake?"

"The Adirondacks."

"And what sort of phenomena has raised the specter of a ghost?"

"During the digging, some bones were unearthed. Apparently, there is an old Indian burial ground under part of the excavation site. The latest incident has been, what I feel is an exaggerated account, of a shaking of the ground and ripples in the lake."

"Pretty tame stuff sounds to me."

"Exactly."

"Were you there when any of these events happened?"

"No. From what I hear, and this is fabricated rubbish as far as I am concerned, there is some tortured history of the lake that goes far back."

"Such as?"

"Such as unusual accidents and not readily understood disappearances."

"All seems rather vague."

"Exactly. If you would just come there for a couple of days and do your thing and issue a report giving a rational explanation to it all, with such a clean bill of health we can get this show back on the road." While he really knew better, he blurted out, "There are millions of dollars at stake here."

The quick-minded professor picked up on the dangling thread immediately. "It will be an expensive effort for me to do this. My calendar is tight and my time and energy are extremely costly. Want to hear more?"

He gulped, knowing full well the tables had been turned against him and that he was proverbially against a stone wall. "Just the bottom line."

"$10,000 a day for me plus travel expenses, and an additional amount for the administrative expense of my assistant who will write the report. That might well be in the thousands. There can be a prompt interim report but a formal final report will take a bit of time and be another $10,000."

"Our money is all tied up in this project. If you will agree to a cap of $50,000 and wait a year from the issuance of the report for receipt of payment, I'll talk it over with my partners and let you know tomorrow. But, you will have to do this next week. We just cannot lose any more time on this. Before we know it winter will be here and nothing will get done."

"Get back to me, and by then I will have reviewed my own impressions of the feasibility of the undertaking."

As the taxi carried Frank away from the university grounds, he already knew that the $50,000 was a necessary expenditure. How many others would arise to dissipate the pursuit of the golden egg?

Christine Longfellow spent some precious moments reviewing the meeting with Frank Lancaster. She already knew that she would take on the investigation not because she was greedy but because the money represented a form of escape for her. Scant returns from her academic accomplishments only forecast a long string of empty years ahead of class schedules and tedious, monotonous writings. She was tired, burned out really, and yearned for a complete alteration of her life. Too young to retire, too old to adapt to a new profession, she longed for the benefits of retirement in concept, or more aptly the freedom it represented. She wanted to try different things, meet new people, far from a college environment. Even if she lacked the talent, she wanted to paint. She looked longingly out of the office window at the broad expanse of the University quadrangle. She did not see individually the grass, the trees, the benches along the pathways, or even the statues. What did only come to her mind was how she might place it all in a painting. This proposal just dropped into her lap was an opportunity to be free.

If the truth were known, she could probably fit a painting of her life on one canvas. Her much older sister had left the family when she was just a baby, and she grew up for all intents and purposes as an only child. Being an only child seems to produce one of two results. Too much attention leads to a spoiled nature; too little involvement equals a nonconfident misfit. There had been no participatory action in her growing years at home. Her intellectual parents treated her as an object of study and to run tests on. No wonder her imaginary companions took on lives of their own. That most likely led to her absorption with and about ghostly things. It also made her withdraw into herself, explaining a lack of friendships. Romantic interludes in the growing years and after that were scarce, and the few that crossed her pathway were of the superficial variety. Considering herself a feeling and emotional person, the lack of human closeness was hard to bear. Perhaps such might have infringed on her association with the strange phenomena she was drawn to and had an uncanny inclination towards. At the age of fifty-two, her life was not set in stone. It was stuck in mud.

She was also extremely impatient and showed little tolerance for stupidity and laziness. That would explain why she had gone through so many assistants. Not one had lasted more than a year. So, to facilitate the process she started to use students affording them extra academic credit. That way, neither she nor the students expected any arrangements to be long lasting. At present, she had one of her brightest students, Ann Farrell, who helped her with the paper work. Christine would go alone to Thumb Lake for a preliminary overview and assessment, and if a follow up was deemed necessary she would then take Ann with her to record and organize notes if a tape recorder was not helpful. If they agreed to her terms, Frank

31

Lancaster would get what he was seeking, and she would take hold of her future.

FIVE

As Christine pulled her car in front of the Skybridge Motel, she felt a bit reluctant to proceed. Far from the lap of luxury, she only hoped that the room and diner were cleaner than the outside appearance. Well-maintained flowers and shrubbery were an interesting contrast, and once again her mind was drawn to look at this as a potential painting. Even the figure of the motel owner, Abner Kressky, would be of further interest as he fit into the setting. Far from the academic types she was surrounded by at the University, Abner was a symbol of the country. He was handsome in his own gruff way, and friendly eyes had put her at ease immediately. His daughter who ran the diner was also refreshingly non-conformist, and after a discussion with her she was also non-complex. Christine was also surprised and delighted at the quality of the food. Overall, it sharpened a different kind of hunger that she had, a thirst for the simple life.

Driving down the narrow road to *Paradise Gardnes* was a totally different issue. With the steep terrain on one side and the lake on the other, a lake the likes of which she had not seen before, an uneasy sensation clutched at her stomach. The lake was foreboding, dark and uninviting. The placid surface was deceptive, and it almost seemed as she drove along that the lake was following her.

Reaching the deserted construction site, her perceptiveness took in the natural beauty of the place. The would-be painter in her absorbed the colors and shapes. Yet, lurking in the backdrop was a dark aura despite the bright sunny day. Perhaps it was just the overall dominance of the mountains that cast a disproportionate height to the yet-to-be-built project. The construction equipment lay abandoned, and piles of dirt and partially dug holes lay like corpses in the dust. The click of her camera was the only sound. The absence of birds added an eerie spell. Dealing over the years with fear-generating features, she had become impervious to the wayward emotion. She was not afraid now, even though she was alone and any cry for help would go unheard and unanswered. Her intellect convinced her that there was nothing evil about the place even if an unsettled pall hung over it. But, if one's mind was prone to thoughts of a haunting, this was the kind of scene and fertile atmosphere to spawn imaginary happenings. These were her initial impressions, and she would come again tomorrow to take a more precise look and study it all anew. A few pointed questions to Abner and Becky might launch a constructive approach to the report she would prepare.

The diner was empty. At the sound of the bell revealing the door being opened or closed, Becky emerged from the kitchen. "Sit where you like, Christine. Meatloaf, mashed potatoes, and fresh peas are just about it. Can you handle it?"

"Actually, it sounds pretty good. I worked up quite an appetite roaming around the construction site. If you have a few minutes later maybe you can fill me in on what you know about the history of the place."

"Pop would be a better source. He knows just about everyone and everything in these parts and has a knack for listenin' to whatever folks talk about. I get bored and tune it all out. My attention span is too short and my memory even shorter. He'll be here soon and I'll have him join you for the vittles."

"Perfect. Thanks, Becky. I might get used to all of this attention. I certainly can get used to your cooking. I live by myself and not even sure I know how to cook. Talk about a short attention span. Probably everything in my kitchen is still brand new."

"Any time you want to join me in the kitchen for some pointers, that'll be fine."

"I might just take you up on that. You may have to start on the basics, such as the difference between a pot and a pan. Maybe I can spice up the report to Mr. Lancaster by adding a couple of your recipes."

"I never follow recipes. It's all thrown together and rarely comes out the same way twice. If it doesn't taste just right, I just add a pinch of this or a smidgen of that."

"Funny. I do the same thing with my reports. If they don't sound just right, I add a bit of extraneous filler here or there. They don't necessarily make any sense but somehow they can tie it all together."

"What are you writing a report on anyway?"

"I am supposed to dispel the alleged strange occurrences that have taken place since they broke ground."

"I have heard fragments of those things. Like everythin' else, everybody has an opinion, right or wrong. Pop, again, is your best authority. We have had a couple of potential buyers stay with us. I am sure they don't know anythin'…yet."

Christine settled into a chair at a table near the kitchen. Once seated, she fully realized how much her feet hurt. It had been awhile since she had worn those heavy hiking boots, specially known for keeping the dampness out and not letting snakebites through. For all of that, they were uncomfortable especially when worn for an extended period of time. She also acknowledged to herself that she was not getting any younger. Before she settled too far into the chair, Becky brought out a plate piled high with her tempting fixings. "Fresh rolls will be out in a jiff."

"I really do like being spoiled."

"No extra charge."

Christine chuckled. "The best kind of spoiled. Now, if I could only take off these darned boots."

"Hey, this is the country. You do as you like, others need to like what you do or skin their own mule."

"Mighty fancy way of saying I can do it." A long sigh of relief as she unlaced the boots and wiggled her toes in the heavy socks.

The food sure was good, and her thoughts flittered away as she became enchanted with each delicious morsel. The warmth of the food settled comfortably in her stomach. Abner's entrance brought her back to this time and place. He sure did cut an imposing figure, and there was an additional warmth spreading on her insides. It had been a long time since she had looked at a man with lustful thoughts peaking in her mind. She motioned for him to join her.

Abner looked at Christine, and for a moment thoughts of Glenda dissipated. Christine was a fine looking woman, and he sure liked how her apparently expensive safari-type outfit clung to her slim frame. For a man whose sexual appetite had been put on hold for a long period, there was a physical and mental rush that kept reminding him that there was plenty of life beyond his small world. Perhaps it was time to grasp at it before it fled beyond his reach.

Abner sat in a chair beside her rather than across from her. The gesture was emphasized and pleased them both. "Well, little lady, how was your day at the stompin' ground?"

"It proved interesting. Now that I have a reference point, do you mind if I ask you some questions?"

"I'm a country bumpkin, as you probably already figured out. I don't know what a reference point is, but I can't really talk until I get some of Becky's vittles into my gut."

"A reference point is just a fancy way of giving the impression that I may know what I am talking about. You eat away. I am packing this in and enjoying every morsel."

"I wish Becky would marry. Her husband would have to come here to live though. I can't do without her cookin'."

"I'd marry her myself just for her cooking, and I could live here just to paint." The statement just came out of her mouth without really thinking about it. Rather unusual for her to say something without a prethought and preapproval from her brain. She had never considered herself a lesbian but many probably supposed she was.

The statement also caught Abner by surprise. He thought better than to respond immediately, and called out to Becky for a giant plate of

36

fixings. After making a significant dent in the heaping pile before him, his remark was innocent by his standards. "I never met a woman who preferred other women to men. Don't get me wrong, I don't judge it."

Christine smiled broadly knowing that his squirming in his chair was a sign that this was a topic he was either not comfortable with or not accustomed to. "I was just jesting. Becky's food is so good I would probably consider any extreme measure to guarantee a steady diet of it. I'd even marry you to get close to her cooking and to paint here unrestrained, God forgive me. My preference is for men but there are a scarce supply of good men."

"You ever been married?"

"No. No time for it and no opportunity. What man would want a woman who deals with ghosts, witchcraft and the like?"

"My wife was a witch. Left us, she did. Only a witch would do that."

"I suppose that is one criteria."

"When you said you would marry me, was that a proposal?" A sheepish grin appeared between his whiskers.

"It was, but you had only ten seconds to accept. Your time has expired."

"Shucks! I can't play by the rules if I do not know 'em."

"It's a good thing for you. You would not know what you would be getting yourself in for."

"Listen, lady, I am no prize package either. I'm just an ole buzzard with a run-down motel that never has and probably never will make a profit."

"That may be true but you fail to see the not-so-apparent treasures. You forget, I am trained to see that. Since I come from and exist in a sort of sterile environment, you have yourself, your daughter, the beauty and peace of this glorious surrounding nature, and you have a pace of life when seconds are precious instead of it all being a blend of inseparable moments."

"Whatever that means. Dull and borin' Becky would say."

"And, dear man, what is so wrong with dull and boring? Excitement is short-lived and shallow."

"Would you really trade your life at the University and your profession for a life like this?"

"As I just said, if I could paint and be near her culinary art, I would do it in a heartbeat."

"Interestin' outlook. I've never met anyone like you."

"Likewise."

He grinned. "Maybe the start of a beautiful friendship."

"Maybe." She gobbled down the last remnants of food from her plate. "What can you tell me about what is going on at *Paradise Gardens?*"

He cleaned off his plate, leaned back, and gazed deeply into the hazel eyes before him. Her glasses could not hide a luster in them that he could not recall ever seeing in a woman's eyes before. He knew he would struggle to recapture that image in his many forthcoming lonely hours. "I'll tell you what I know, at least what I think I know. Tomb Lake has always been a mystery. You can talk to a dozen folks hereabouts and you'll get twelve different stories, even twelve different variations of the same story. People see and hear what they think they want to see or hear, or even what they are told to see and hear. My father, who started this motel, even back then, told me never to go there. He said bad things happen at that lake. But, I did go more out of bein' a contrary little cuss than for any other reason. The water is too cold for swimmin', I never heard of anyone catchin' a fish there, and the ground is hard and hilly. Not a youthful attraction. Even in high school, the few guys who had cars would not go there to park and neck with the girls because the road was bumpy and hard on the cars. The girls were afraid to go there anyway. There is no shortage of secluded spots in the country. Those people who might have gone to the lake for picnics or who hauled boats there, all had some complaints to make. Wind would come up all of a sudden, and it would whistle down the mountainsides so loud you could not hear talkin'. Vines smothered out any hikin' trails, and a gloom hung over spots where folks spread their blankets. When the wind was not makin' noise, it was too quiet, so they say. Even the scenic views lost appeal when one keeps lookin' over your shoulder. Know what

I mean?"

"I noticed that today. I didn't see or hear any birds."

"Then, there would be the tales of a mossy film on the water and a stench not unlike rottin' bodies. It gave the storytellers a field day. Some disappearances, unexplained and probably never to be explained, gave further inspiration to horror stories." He wanted to tell her about the Lancaster brothers and the incomplete and unrealistic plans for the project, but since he needed the business that might loom ahead he held back. After all, that was unrelated to her reason for being here. When the time was right, he would say his piece.

"Are there any descendants from the Indian tribes who were here?"

"A few further down from here. They are loners and never come up this way any more. I never met any of them, although there's many a story about 'em."

"Is there a local library?"

"No. Mrs. Peabody has a couple of hundred books she lets folks use, and the public library is in the next county."

"Are there any written histories of the town?"

"Not that I know of. You can ask Mrs. Peabody. I think she is about a hundred years old and feeble, but who knows what writings she has on her shelves. Maybe she will let you take a look see."

"I will let you take me to see her when and if."

"Are you goin' over to the site tomorrow?"

"Yes."

"Would you like me to go with you?"

"I would like that very much."

SIX

The Pruitts received back a completely signed copy of the agreement. Yet, they thought it a bit odd when they called to request a follow-up visit to the site that they were told to wait a few weeks because blasting was taking place. They had noted that the roads were completed and the construction holes apparently all in place. It did not make sense but they did not want to dwell on it. The delay in seeing Abner and Becky was the real discordant note. The young are impatient for love; older people are desperate once they get a taste of it.

Glenda called Abner from her office just about every weekday. It surprised her that they found so much to talk about since their backgrounds and frames of reference were so diverse. Just listening to the deep resonance of his voice put her at ease. It made her think of a boy friend she had in high school. They had talked on the telephone every night, often for hours at a time. They talked about everyone and everything. Impressions and expressions ran the full gamut from what then seemed so simple to the complex. That relationship had come to an abrupt end. Looking back on it now, she could not recall why she had given up such an absorbing situation.

Abner made her giggle the way she used to before the crush of a serious life descended upon her. It was the absence of any inhibitions which pleased her the most. Not only was this a refreshing change from her married situation, it was also in sharp contrast to the strict demands of her job. Once removed from such confines, it was surprisingly delightful to feel unrestrained. It was a rediscovery of her true self. A twinge of regret seared her soul that she had given up that personal space by virtue of the confines of job and marriage. Glenda had no way of knowing that a competitor for Abner's affections had arrived on the scene. If she knew, it might have made Abner even more desirable.

As for Dwight, the thoughts of Becky gave him a brighter and more energetic outlook. There was no telephone at the diner, and they talked only a couple of times when she made her way to the motel office to call him. He had encouraged her to call at any time, and he instructed his secretary that such calls were of the utmost importance and she should interrupt him to take the calls no matter what other involvement had his attention. He could only imagine what lewd thoughts were going through the secretary's mind. At some earlier point in time that might have affected him. Now, he did not care in the least what others thought of him and what he did. He had spent too much of his life looking backwards. A new horizon had opened before him and he was dead set on reaching any potential it might offer.

As Dwight leaned back in his desk chair, he swiveled around so he could peer out of the window into the dingy haze surrounding the Manhattan buildings, and he did something he had not done in a very long time. He analyzed his earlier life. There had been one substantial, albeit remarkable, turning point in his life. He was an only child, ignored by the circumstances of his successful parents who owned a retail operation and were swept up in it six days a week. He had no confidence, was awkward and unaggressive. He was timid at school, barely progressing in an average way. After the early years when the family sent him with an aunt and uncle for the summers up at Schroon Lake where he loved it, he was sent to summer camp each year, and he hated it since he was a poor athlete and barely tolerated by his more animated and talented bunkmates. The camp was in Connecticut and most of the campers would congregate at Grand Central Station for the train ride to the village near the camp. Two buses would take them from the station to the camp. Other campers arrived by other means from various destinations, even as far away as Florida.

When he was fourteen, that summer as he waited at Grand Central

Station for the counselors to line them up for entry to the train platform, he noticed two young girls in the group looking over the crowd and then staring at him. One girl was rather tall and the other on the short and stocky side. Even over the din, he noticed the shorter girl pointing at him and heard her say, "He is kind of cute." As was almost a camp ritual, they were prearranging who their boyfriends would be for the summer. He had long since forgotten her name, and her face was fuzzy in his memory. But, one thing he did remember vividly. She had the largest bosoms for such a small girl. It turned out that she had the largest chest size in the camp, even larger than any of the female counselors. On the first Saturday night social in the hall above the boat dock, when she approached him and asked him to dance and thrust out those lovely chest adornments and pressed them against him, and then not letting go of him all of the social period as well as for the entire summer, he became a camp legend. The next day when she held his hand at the lake wearing a skimpy bathing suit, he was the talk and admiration of every boy at the camp. The quiet child emerged overnight as a conquering hero, a trait that carried him through to become a successful bankruptcy attorney. It was the quality that he used successfully to woo Glenda who was from an elitist family and sought after by many other suitors. He was on a fast track for a prominent tomorrow, and she was the proper accompaniment.

It was also the trait that Glenda had found so beguiling. As an intelligent and attractive young woman from a prominent Long Island family, she recognized in Dwight the potential for a successful and financially secure future. She thought the comfort level would grow into love, but it never really did. Romance was pure emotion to her and strictly business for him. As the years drifted by and an all-encompassing involvement in careers left no time or incentive for children, to her total dismay she awakened one day to realize that even if she wanted children she was beyond a safe child-bearing age. They had talked about adoption, but the demanding career paths appeared to carry them further and further away from a family scenario. Years passed without escape. Just when change appears remote, shifting sands can alter the landscape.

SEVEN

The first debate at breakfast was whose car to take. Abner offered his beat up truck just in case they might venture off the beaten track. Christine won out after pointing out she might need some of the equipment kept in her car. Becky packed them a box lunch, and off they went.

Abner stared at the swell of her breasts through the kaki shirt as she drove. The pants fit snugly over shapely legs. Her profile revealed a sharp nose beneath the glasses, full cheeks, perky lips, and a creamy complexion. A sheen added an allure to her short brown hair, and he surmised that she was younger than he had first guessed. He also gazed at her hands on the steering wheel. The long, tapered fingers were beguiling, nearly mesmerizing. Yes, after a long dry spell, Abner was immersed in more than he knew he could handle. Two potential loves, a double dilemma.

She caught his fixed gaze. "Are you studying me?"

He was never a person to hold back. "Yeah. And I like what I see."

"What do you see other than an old frump?"

"I don't have your education and can only guess what a frump is. There are plenty of folks out there who will tear you down. No sense in doin' it to yourself."

"Saves time and energy that way."

"I like what I see. You're an interestin' lookin' woman. Sexy, too."

She shot a sideways look at him. "Better study me closer. I'm an intellect and no hot chick."

"The two can't mix?"

"It has always been that way. Men, what few of them are worth

45

associating with, have only been interested in my mind."

"They are fools I would say. Your body, even under wraps, sure seems fetchin' to me."

"Maybe you are the fool."

"Even a fool is entitled to a shinin' moment, an instant to enjoy the spotlight."

"Quite prophetic for a mountain man."

"Pathetic, you say?"

"Profound"

"Stop usin' them fancy words, otherwise I will have to fall for your mind as well as your body."

"I don't think I have ever met anyone quite like you."

"Is that good or bad?"

"Too soon to tell. Just keep saying those nice things and I just might want to get to know you."

At that moment they pulled onto the construction site. She parked the car by what was the original gate. "Let's walk from here. We'll make a sweep around and work our way down to the lake."

Christine opened the trunk and pulled out a weird looking instrument and retrieved the camera from the back seat. A small hand-held tape recorder rounded out the equipment needed for the investigation. She handed the instrument to Abner. "Here, you may carry this, able assistant."

"What is it?"

"A ghost-o-meter."

"Wow!"

"Several years ago a colleague of mine developed it. Quite ingenious it is. There are three gauges. One measures vibrations, another can pick up high-pitched noises the human ear cannot hear, and the third can detect the slightest changes in light patterns."

"Sounds like a love-o-meter to me."

"You old birds have a one-track mind."

"It's the only way to get from here to there."

She turned the instrument on and handed it to him. In silence they walked around the grounds. The crew would not return until she reported on the absence of a haunting. It was far better they were not disturbed. No distraction to deter her concentration or to give false readings on the machine. The initial tour the day before led her to concentrate on certain areas, and to linger at spots where some uncertainty might exist. Nothing broke the silence, and her initial impression of the absence of birds was reinforced, although she was not sure what the reason might be.

By the time they had made their way down to the lake, none of the gauges had budged. Abner kept a dutiful eye on the needles, with an occasional glance towards this most interesting woman. He sure liked the way she moved with grace and confidence. It was probably a good thing the instrument could not measure the increased pace of his heartbeat.

Christine stopped before the lake and took in the full panorama of the natural beauty of the place. "Sure makes me want to paint what I see. I have always had the urge to paint, and the desire is getting stronger the older I get. A day will come when I will put all of this nonsense behind me and just paint to my heart's content. Whether I am good at it or not, I do believe the release and involvement is my dream. I even find your motel an interesting subject for a picture."

"That would be a first," Abe said with a grin. "Most people can't wait to get the place out of their sight, and probably the last place they ever want to remember."

"I guess it is part of my training and experience. I see beyond what others may see." She sat on a rock near the water's edge. "I am getting a bit thirsty."

He put the instrument down besides her. "It has been a couple of hours. I am goin' back to the car to get the drinks and sandwiches Becky made for us. We'll have a picnic, and knowin' Becky there'll be extra food for any ghosts that show up."

While he was gone, she studied the water and the surrounding terrain. Small ripples spread out as far as she could see, and the ripples distorted the reflections of the mountains and the trees. One could wonder whether we ever see what we are meant to see, or whether all of our views are merely reflections in troubled waters. It was difficult for her to concentrate as thoughts of Abe intruded on the intellectual patterns she was trying to establish. How long had it been since she had felt such a strong attraction for a man? Interestingly, it was not just a physical attraction. She sensed his sincerity and with his attentive mannerism she felt comfortable with him. Even talking to him was easy. That in itself spoke volumes.

It turned out that Abe was a peanut butter and jelly sandwich fiend, having that staple nearly every day for lunch. Christine laughed robustly as she declared that it was also her favorite lunchtime indulgence. She would make the creation the night before so that the jelly would adequately permeate into the bread. A favorite variation was to add sliced cucumber. So, as they munched on the pbj's and drank the iced tea, a mutual culinary delight was shared and it added another note of satisfaction with each other's company. An extension of no pretension. The fresh brownies were delectable morsels. A knowing smile capped the warm feeling as if two youngsters were sharing a close and forbidden secret.

She took a series of pictures of the lake and surrounding terrain. Observations were dictated into the recorder, and after two more hours they headed back to the motel. They stopped a few times along the lake's length so that she could take some more pictures. The day had been uneventful from a ghost hunter perspective. The day had been a memorable one for two lonely people. The significance of a moment can be quite personal and perpetual.

Back in the motel room, she played back her recordings and wrote some extensive notes of the impressions she had, and in her mind she had reached a tentative conclusion both about the mystery of the lake as well as about Abe. One last trip to the lake tomorrow should be definitive on both scores. The day after she had to return to the University.

They ate supper together, feasting on Becky's sumptuous meat loaf. Becky sat with them for a spell as there were few customers. Perhaps, it was

48

because of the ominous sky that opened up with torrential rain. Maybe, it was because the word had spread, which it often does in rural communities quickly and embellished, that a ghost hunter was there. Witchcraft is still witchcraft even if it may wind up being beneficial.

After Christine left for her room, Becky lingered at the table with her father. "Well, Pop, what is Casanova up to now?"

"Nothin' gets by you, does it little girl?"

"It's as if you were a doormat for a long time and now the volcano is eruptin' full force. I doubt if you can handle two woman, much less one."

"Sure might be fun to try. Which one do you like better?"

"Don't get me involved in your mess."

"Jus' a little opinion, gal."

"No opinions, no choices, but I do have some advice for you. Even a beast can tackle too much."

He chuckled. "A beast finally set free needs to roam."

"Just remember that beasts are also part of the food chain. There are larger forces out there that can devour you in an instant."

"I'd give him indigestion."

"A beast that is also a tough bird. What a dangerous combination!"

"And you are a sweet bird. When are you gonna fly free?"

"One of us has to have some sense. I won't fly free until I can fly right."

RESTLESS BEAUTY

EIGHT

Even his swanky office on Madison Avenue had lost its attractiveness. When he first occupied it after several years in a cramped hole on First Avenue he was thrilled beyond words. His loyal customer base had encouraged him to update his surroundings to entice a more high-end clientele. It was a risk, yet he was young and eager and knew that his talent met the level of his undertakings. Success had come early and gave him the security and confidence to lead others to new bounds. No longer need he be envious of what others might have or what they might do. He was the leader of the pack. Yet, even that kind of euphoria fades without any deeper personal value. After the recent fortieth birthday party held by his staff for him at a top-rated New York restaurant, he had walked the streets feeling anew a loneliness and emptiness that comes with being busy but not enjoying the accomplishments. Money, prominence and leadership can become in a way as draining as failure. The bevy of beautiful women who sought him out, while exciting and ego lifting in the beginning, now paled in the guise of sameness. The haunting question that had formed in his mind reverberated to his very core. *Grady Reighton, what do you really want out of life?*

Being a financial advisor to a long list of clients who depended on him for their well-being, he was always on the lookout for unusual investment opportunities. That is why he had kept the slick brochure on *Paradise Gardens*. It lay on the corner of his desk periodically staring up at him. He had been around long enough to be wary of such enticing overtures, knowing full well that they often were just a beguiling come-on without true substance to back them up. Yet, this venture struck him as something to look into for

51

several reasons. Real property was still a good investment. Water view and access properties always had and always will have a special appeal, as there were just so much around with those attributes. Mountain property was also an additional draw and another instance of diminishing supply. The combination of those positives added a value that might be highly rewarding in the long-term.

Whenever possible, Grady tried to check out such potential investments personally. That way he could get the best feel for the possibilities and genuinely be able to recommend it to his clients enthusiastically. That was the kind of service they were used to from him and expected. So, checking on this endeavor might be a good business prospect, as well as affording him a temporary break from the stultifying situations crushing in around him. It was always a major production to rearrange his schedule to clear time for a trip although his staff could always carry on for a short spell as long as they could communicate with him if needed.

When he called the toll-free telephone number, he was told he would have to wait for a couple of weeks to visit the site due to construction blasting but that the free stay nearby would still be available. He was hoping for a quicker escape. Giving him something to look forward to was a tolerable alternative.

Due south in Greenwich Village, Colleen McKenzie was just finishing her third cup of morning coffee as she sat before her computer in the small apartment where the books she wrote came alive. It was a good thing that those stories had an existence because she did not have one. The first three books had been generally favorably reviewed but royalties were quite meager. Life was a struggle while she immersed herself in her writing forsaking friends and social situations. Today was her thirty-sixth birthday. Nobody remembered that, she was sure. Her mother used to make such occasions special but with her death two years ago the one person was gone who was capable of making her day a celebration rather than a dismal reminder of her growing old in an empty life. So, the heroines in her books, flashy commercial successes, lived the life she wished for herself, filled with excitement, wealth and love. Each glamorous woman was personable and brilliant, with business acumen a natural attribute. These were the features she dreamt for herself. There was always a beautiful and satisfying romantic involvement, a scenario totally lacking and promising to be forever absent in her life. Happy endings for the books which seemed to be a natural aftermath for those productive and fortunate individuals only added to her own personal gloom. For her, there had been no memorable romantic involvements, and the characters in her books would have to live the life she was being denied. While she was rather plain in appearance and dull in personality, there was no problem bestowing superlative qualities on the women in the stories. The writing was the conceptualization of her aspirations, and it was the only thing that stood in the way of total depression. The walls of the tiny place she called home closed in on her, and scrimping on food was tiresome and debilitating. A daily walk only accentuated her abject posture. Beautiful and lively people passed her in the streets or congregated with laughter in the outdoor cafes that lined the quaint streets. Not a soul acknowledged her presence, and as a shadow she moved silently heading to nowhere.

On this particular day, a late summer drizzle enfolded the narrow streets, and it was a source of refreshment to feel the fine mist hit her enflamed face as she walked. To her surprise, there was a birthday card in her mailbox. She waited until she was upstairs before opening it. The card was from her Aunt Christine, her mother's much younger sister, now a professor at the State University. She had rarely seen her, although she had always admired her accomplishments and read all of her books. She was not sure that she had fully grasped the discussions of the findings of what others called unexplainable. As her aunt dealt with the fear engendered by the unknown, her own torment was based on what she knew her limited existence entailed. In the back of her mind a seed was germinating to incorporate her aunt's special talents for a protagonist in a future book.

Aunt Christine had been at her mother's funeral but they had exchanged only a few cordial words. She reread the aunt's comments in the card and wondered what might become of them. *Colleen, dear, I meant to talk with you in more detail at the funeral. I promised your mother that I would stay close to you. Time is my worst enemy, and please consider this a way overdue initial effort for me to be in contact with you. I have read and enjoyed your books. Your sweet talent is so reflective of your mother's secret desires. I will make room for you in my world if you care to branch out. Call me when you are able. The number is here on the card I am enclosing. Hugs, Aunt Christine*

Anxious to thank her for the card and curious to know why after all of these years she now remembered her birthday, Colleen called the direct number on the card. The call was channeled to Ann Farrell, her aunt's assistant. Ann told her that Christine was away in the mountains investigating some strange occurrences there and would be back the day after tomorrow. She would be sure to have her return the call.

At about the same time, the telephone rang on Gail Cohen's desk at the New York State Attorney General's Fraud Division. Her supervisor, Joe Stockman, asked her to come to his office. As a recent law graduate, admitted to the bar on the first take of the bar examination, at age twenty-seven she was a bright legal star. Shunning the corporate legal world and private law firm prospects, she had opted for this civil service post so she could help people close to home.

Joe looked at this enthusiastic young woman seated before his desk, wishing he could recapture that youthful spirit that had waned so long ago under the heavy burden of managerial responsibility. "Gail, I have a really interesting assignment for you. It involves some field investigation. Are you up to it?"

Gail smiled, brushing back the straight black hair from the edge of her face. "I'm ready if you think I am up to it."

"Believe me, I wouldn't give it to you if I had any doubts about you handling it. It will get you some time out of the office too. We don't do as much field work as we used to but I have always believed it is invaluable." He handed her a file. "Everything you need to know is here. The Florida AG has sent everything they have on Harold and Frank Lancaster. They have been involved in some shady deals in Florida and have now moved some of their operations up north to us and have undertaken a project in the Adirondacks. It may be legit, but considering their past history it could just be an elaborate scam. They have ripped off folks before. After you study this, clear yourself a few days to go there and check it out. I have set up an expense account for you. Just keep a record of all you spend and submit it through me when you return. I will be anxious to hear what you find. If nothing else, it will be good to put the Lancasters on notice that we are watching them."

At her desk, Gail carefully reviewed the contents of the file twice just to make sure she had a full grasp of it all. Never hearing of Thumb Lake, she checked the map and found a Tomb Lake. That is interesting, she thought with a grimace. Then, she checked out the area on her computer, finding only one motel in the vicinity. She dialed the Skybridge Motel, waiting seven rings before it was answered by a man with a deep voice and an apparent local dialect. After identifying herself she made a reservation for two days two weeks from now. The man never even asked her why she was coming there. She could be wrong, but she had the distinct feeling that he knew.

Later that evening, after dinner with her parents and two teenage brothers, Gail tossed and turned most of the night. Here she was on her own and yet still living with her parents at the family home. That security was the backbone of who she was. However, there was some trepidation about the forthcoming investigation. It was important that she handle it just right. She was not worried about her own professionalism although there was some extended effort needed to make that apparent to a group of strangers. Was it too tall an order for a young and relatively inexperienced attorney? She probably could not have arranged a better test of her resolve than this. Little wonder there was some anxiety gnawing at her insides. At times, the future is not measured in terms of years. It may be gauged in weeks.

NINE

Christine and Abner left for the construction area right after breakfast. Rebecca thought it odd that Christine asked that a couple of plain pieces of bread be included in the peanut butter and jelly picnic lunch. Her association with intellects had been scant so she just figured after accepting it that each had a peculiarity as in the end they are different from most folks. She would not interfere with her father's life, although she had been tempted to answer when he had asked her which woman she favored that it was Christine. Glenda was a married woman that had its own complications. Becky sensed that Christine was a more patient and less demanding person. She also liked the soft tones that Christine used when she spoke to her father. Her laugh also seemed more genuine. Becky knew she was not the best judge of character but this is the way it looked to her.

Christine turned the car motor off when they parked by the lake. She turned to Abe and put her hand on his arm. She felt the taut muscle through the fabric of the flannel shirt. "Before we start, I would like you to do me a favor."

"Gladly, lass."

"Will you kiss me?"

Not used to surprises, this one he could handle. He leaned towards her, clasped her hands and kissed her tenderly on the lips. He noted a slight trembling in the lips. A second kiss was more ardent as he enfolded her in his powerful arms. "Any more favors?"

"One more, please. Can you come to my room tonight?"

This was another delightful surprise. "Sure enough, little lady. It is

57

you that will be doin' me the favor."

Another unexpected request came when she opened the trunk and asked him to bring the ghost-o-meter, a shovel, two empty glass vials, and the two pieces of bread from the picnic basket. He could not contain his curiosity. "What is the shovel for?"

"Just in case you decide to bombard me with flowery expressions of affection, I can dig my way out."

"I should've guessed that. And the bread? A condemned man's last supper?"

"You'll see. All in due time."

Christine took the bread, broke it into pieces and threw it out onto the water. No fish came for the feast. There were no minnows and no tadpoles at the water's edge. The reflections at the surface of the lake had no uniform pattern, and some were much brighter than others. She took a sample of the water in one of the vials. She then asked Abe to dig a couple of holes. No ants, no worms, nothing. She took a soil sample in the other vial.

She asked him to keep a sharp lookout for any kind of wildlife as they circled the property. For the entire time they were there, there was not a single sighting and no abnormal readings on the machine.

As they sat on the embankment to partake in the lunch, Abe asked innocently, "What do you make of all of this?"

"I'm really not sure. I will have to dwell on it. Do you have any birds and squirrels at the motel?"

"Yeah. Too many. Freeloaders at the feeders, and lots of butterflies at the bushes. Even snakes, mostly garter snakes. How come there are none here?"

"I have never seen anything like this before. Of course, to some extent the construction activity and especially the noise may have frightened some of the animals away. That would not explain an absence of fish in the lake. Maybe, something toxic was dumped in the water, but there are no fish bodies to indicate that. We'll have to see what analysis of the samples reveals. In the meantime, it is a real mystery."

"You're one smart cookie."

"Not smart enough to avoid getting involved with you."

"That, lass, is the smartest thing you can do."

"That remains to be seen."

"Just don't be too quick to judge."

"You should already know that I don't rush to any kind of decision."

They had supper together. Becky's beef stew was completely satisfying and even though tired they talked and stared at each other like young lovers. Rebecca grinned each time she caught a glimpse of their animated behavior. Her father had always been precious to her, and never more endearing as at this moment seeing him laugh and having a woman pay special attention to him. If this worked out for him, she would be very happy for him. A time might even draw near when she could concentrate on her future before that possibility was beyond control.

Shortly after nine, Christine answered the light knock at the door. The nightgown she wore was matronly but that had been the design and purpose of her wardrobe. Abner still gasped when he saw her, the lamp behind her giving a pronounced outline to the feminine form beneath the fabric. He embraced her as he kicked the door closed behind him. Still locked in one another's arms they drifted towards the bed.

After gentle lovemaking, they fell into a peaceful sleep holding on firmly, exhaustion from the day daunting the spirit of wakeful togetherness. It was a memorable night for them in their individual ways, prompting a mutuality that can only be aspired to. The true meaning would settle into their lives as they relived the experience.

As Christine drove off in the morning towards the college, tears formed at the corners of her eyes. If only she could paint the beauty she was feeling. Abe stared longingly after her even after the car disappeared around the bend. In the sameness that had held him captive for so many years, it took only one night to give birth to an upheaval.

TEN

It was early afternoon when Christine arrived at her university office. As much as she preferred not to, she had to put her personal euphoria aside to concentrate on getting out a preliminary report right away so that Frank Lancaster would not balk at carrying out his end of the deal. She was glad she had it all in writing and it loomed even larger for her in the light of recent developments.

Timing worked out just right as Ann had just come to the office from her last class for the day. She was a rather frail woman, and Christine often felt bad about burdening her with work. Yet, her intelligence and flare for organization saved Christine from herself. It was obvious that in addition to the credits she needed the salary that Christine paid her, and there would be a bonus too when Christine received her payment from the Lancasters.

"Hi, Ann," she expounded with enthusiasm.

"Hello yourself. The mountain air must have agreed with you. You look really good."

"Just getting away from here works wonders."

Ann thought to herself that she would not be that lucky, and probably never will be, as riches appear to be a vague vision for her life. "No doubt."

"Please take these two samples to the Jessup Lab and ask them for an analysis. Tell them it's a rush, which still means we'll have to wait a good ten days. We just don't have that kind of time. I want to fax a preliminary report to Mr. Lancaster tomorrow. By the time you get back from the lab,

I will have an outline of the major points for the report, and you can add the usual fluff. By the time we get the lab report I will have all of the pictures I took developed, and the final report hopefully will just all be a confirmation of the preliminary findings. Keep your fingers crossed. Sound alright by you?"

Ann sighed, and she knew it would be a long night. It was a good thing that she enjoyed doing this. If nothing else, it took her mind off of her own problems. "Sure enough. It was too quiet around here while you were gone. Your niece called. Her number is on the pad on your desk."

Ann left in a hurry with the samples, once again congratulating herself on the lucky break to be the professor's assistant. Despite the rumors of how tough she was and that few could stand working for her for any length of time, for a person whose background was nondescript this job would sparkle on her resume. If she could wangle a good letter of recommendation from the professor, that should open doors of opportunity that might not otherwise be available to her.

Christine sat at the desk, noted Colleen's number, and decided to call her after she wrote out the major items for Ann to work her magic on in creating the report. Her inner report on Abe was not going to be shared.

Preliminary conclusion: There appears to be no sinister or unexplainable presence or any mysterious or unknown force in the area of Thumb Lake or the Paradise Gardens construction site. Events as related seem to have a natural, even if unusual, explanation. Any early historical incidents are most likely the result of coincidence or hearsay distortions.

Thorough close personal observations of the construction site and the surrounding area did not reveal any situation warranting undue concern. Scientific measurements of any abnormal activity proved negative.

The lake contains numerous dangerous geological features. The most

62

probable cause of the lake upheaval and the ground tremors was a large rock cliff breaking off and settling heavily on the lake bottom. This would have displaced water at the surface and the impact could well have sent shock waves towards and on the shore, perhaps just beneath the kind of seismic activity that might have been measurable elsewhere even if strong enough to dislodge an old water tower which probably had hidden weaknesses.

The buried bones are undoubtedly Indian relics of animal sacrifices.

Results of analyses of water and soil samples are pending.

At this point, she decided not to bring up the issue of the lack of fish and other wildlife. This was an open question and might be easily answered with the lab reports. It did gnaw at the back of her mind that there were no signs of fish in the lake. After all, Abe did mention that the locals used to fish there, and the three men that disappeared from the cottage colony did so when they were fishing.

After Ann returned, she went to the outer cubicle to begin composing the kind of impressive and substantive reports the professor had a reputation for offering. She was thrilled that the professor put her name on the report covers as her personal assistant.

Christine sat back for a moment, an image of Abe appearing in her mind. Never had her body seemed so alive. As she had promised to do, she called him to inform him that she had arrived safely. Her smile was broad when he told her that he missed her already. The word was magical when she uttered it, "Likewise."

Colleen had been staring at the screen saver on her computer terminal, admonishing herself on another unproductive day. She jumped when the perpetually idle telephone rang. "Hello."

"Hello, dear. It is Aunt Christine."

"Thanks for the birthday card. It is a really nice card. I sure was surprised to get it."

"I was remiss in not sending one last year. Your mother was quite a bit older than me, as you know, and because of that extreme difference in our ages, we were never close growing up. In the six months before her death, that changed. She continued to make overtures to me. She knew she was about to die and wanted to make up to me for any slight she thought came my way. I never did blame her or hold anything against her. We spoke on the telephone often. One of her deepest concerns was about you. One of her repeated requests was for me to remember your birthdays. She loved you very much. As our closeness developed I had new regrets about not knowing you better. We are our only relatives."

"Yes, I know. Mom started to talk more about you before her death. I have always admired you, and have even read all of your books."

"Ah, and so have I read yours. They are fine works and you have a special talent. My preoccupation leads to an uncanny perceptiveness. I get the impression that your books are only the kind of life you would like to have."

"Sadly, true."

"Are you having financial problems as well?"

"Yes. It is a struggle."

"That can add greater enormity to other issues."

"I do not need your pity. Somehow, I will manage."

"I do not pity you. I just want you to know that I understand that there can be a large gap between doing and having. My life has reached a turning point. I was always sure I would be ready for it when it came. Now, I am actually afraid of it."

"Sounds to me that you are lucky to have choices."

"Perhaps. It just is not easy. Hardships come in different packages. Anyway, that is my problem. Actually, I could use your help on this latest investigation I am doing, and by you helping me maybe I can help you."

"How so?" Colleen's suspicious nature raised a red flag of caution.

Christine explained in detail all about the *Paradise Gardens* happenings and her involvement. It was after that she posed the proposition to her niece. "I have completed the field aspect and am issuing a preliminary report. I need somebody to do background research for me for the final report. There is no public library there, but apparently an elderly lady has amassed a collection of whatever local history there is. I'd like you to go up there to interview her and go through the collection for anything relevant. That way all of the bases will be covered, all the corners rounded. No stone unturned. I will pay you a salary and all of your expenses. There is only one place to stay there, it is not fancy but it is clean and the world's best cook prepares meals at the adjoining diner. A subsidiary personal interest is, is that I am a spinster whose final chance at romance may have greeted me. I have been quite taken with the motel owner, Abe, and I would love for him to meet my only relative. I would also be curious about your impression of him. After you spend a couple of days there, I will join you and we can spend some time together. It will give me the chance to see Abe again too."

Colleen grinned. An obvious golden opportunity to break through the doldrums and make some money. "Sounds great."

"I thought it might be appealing. I will mail you a copy of the preliminary report tomorrow with all the other information you will need. I will alert Abe about you."

"Thank you."

"No. Thank you."

Frank Lancaster was elated when Professor Longfellow's preliminary report arrived. *This is just what the doctor ordered.* He wasted no time in getting the report to Jack who immediately contacted each worker explaining what the report said and assuring them that a full copy would be available for reading at the site for those who cared to look at it. The workers agreed to return to work the next day. Some valuable construction days had been lost, but there was still time to get some structures up and under roof before the harsh winter set in. Inside work on those structures could be undertaken throughout the winter. Jack crossed his fingers. His worries were not totally allayed. He still felt uneasy, especially as the responsibility for any further setbacks was to be his to bear. Faulty machinery and fidgety workers do not equal easy or assured progress.

ELEVEN

Glenda hung up the telephone after her daily talk with Abe. Was she imagining it or was there something different about him? He was as cordial as ever but not quite as talkative, and he was very general about what he had been doing. Being in the corporate world for so long, she had become good at noting subtle aspects of business relations. Personal relations would be no different. She hoped she was wrong this time as Abe had prompted a spark of interest and change. It would be disappointing if that lapsed before she could explore the full potential of her new thoughts and feelings. She would know for sure next time she saw him. She sensed that Dwight was also communicating with Becky, and it would be interesting to find out if he had similar impressions about her. They needed to get back up there. Too many loose ends were dangling in the wind.

Later that week, Becky closed up the diner earlier than usual. There had been no customers, the dense fog probably keeping even the most daring close to the hearth. Rarely did she feel sorry for herself, but this particular day she was steeped in her disillusions of days past and the nebulous content of future dreams. Her heart raced at the thought of Dwight but a reality check kept reminding her that their two worlds were basically incompatible. She could no more adapt to the big city than he could to the snail's pace and simplicity of the country. As much as she wanted to be in a different place and doing varied activity, there was no escaping the comfort zone of country life. Perhaps, it was just that the longer she was stuck in this box the more difficult it would be to adjust to being outside of it. The modern concept she heard and read about was that people should think and act out of the box, and yet that was a simple way to preach without a detailed blueprint for a social coward. Maybe it was time she squarely faced her personal inadequacies and learned to just make the most of her shortcomings. After all, she loved her father and she took exceptional pride in her culinary ability even if it grated her at times. Even a relatively empty life can have warm memories. Should that be enough for her? Could it be sufficient to just enjoy meager rewards? She had heard of people stewing in their own juices and often wondered what that really meant. Now she had an inkling of its significance, and she became more determined than ever not to let any negatives rule her life. If this is what she was meant to be and have, that would be her course.

She entered the house weary and yet strangely uplifted. Abner was watching television, his large frame sprawled on the sofa, his usual wool sock feet resting on the ottoman. He clicked the television off with the remote as she sat besides him. She kissed him lightly on the cheek.

"Uh oh, what did I do now?"

"Nothin' dear father. I love you very much, and I do not say it or express it as often as I should."

"That does make an ole man's heart glad, little angel. Especially in light of what demands may soon be made on you."

"Like what?"

"For a couple of stick-in-the-muds, things are gonna take a fast turn around here."

"How so, you ole buzzard?"

"Next week we are pretty much gonna have a full house. Funny, I can't remember a time when we are that busy. Anyway, I'll have to get Matty to get someone else to help her with the housekeeping duties. I know you will be glad to hear, at least, that the Pruitts will be here." He stopped for an instant to note the smile appear on her lips as her eyes widened. "Christine's niece, a writer so she tells me, is comin' to interview Mrs. Peabody and go through her books. This is supposed to help Christine do the final report on the construction area. Next, a lady from the Attorney General's office is comin'. I'm not sure what she is after but it ain't about our motel business. Things could get heated up around here. Then there is a bunch of possible buyers acomin'. One is some kinda financial advisor from New York City. Another is a couple from Syracuse. Also, a retired schoolteacher from Canada is making the trek here. There could be more. Both of the Lancaster boys will be staying with us too. I suppose Frank can't do all the sellin' by himself with this crowd."

"Wow! The Skybridge Motel is a hit. I never thought I'd see that day."

"Me neither, babes. I'm not sure I can get used to it, and I'm not even sure I can count that much money. Sorry that it will mean so much extra cookin' for you."

"Not a problem, ole man. I know it makes no sense, but any cook will tell you that it is actually easier to cook for a bunch than a few. I'll call tomorrow for an extra supply of ingredients."

"Whatever you say, I'm with you."

"Don't expect menu choices, though. They get what I give 'em."

"Works for me. Still will be the best eatin' they ever had."

"If it interferes with any time with Dwight, if that is gonna be such a thing, expect a rebellion in the kitchen."

"If that is what it is, I'll do the cookin'."

"Nobody will ever come back, that is for sure."

"That might get 'em riled up, no doubt. Actually, there may be a whole mess of fireworks, little darlin'."

TWELVE

As it turned out, the entire crowd checked in on the same day. The only ones to show up in the morning were John and Florence Murrow from Syracuse. Both had recently retired, he from banking and she from utility work. In the short time out of the worker ranks they were bored, so when they saw the advertisement for a free stay to tour *Paradise Gardens*, they thought this would be an opportunity to be occupied away at no cost for a couple of days. Nobody need know their true motive, and they were willing to tolerate the sales pitch that would accompany the freebie. After a really satisfying lunch at the diner, they took a short walk and retired to their room for the afternoon.

The first to arrive in the afternoon was Grady Reighton. He had started out early in the morning, his excitement building as he drove along. Anxious to separate himself from his business and city stultification, even the long breaths he took were exhilarating. He stopped once for coffee, and took in all of the vistas along the way. The Skybridge Motel was unlike any motel he had ever seen before, but it would take much more than a run-down place just for sleeping and eating to daunt his newfound freedom.

Just as he pulled in front of the dilapidated building designated as the office, another car pulled in besides his. He went over to it and opened the door for the young woman who smiled at him. When she got out, he noticed how petite she was, nearly fitting a description of dainty. Her features were rather plain and her short brown hair dull and straggly. Yet, there was a glow about her that entranced him. "Hello. I am Grady," he said offering his hand out.

71

She grasped it and shook it with the little strength that she had. "I am Colleen." It was her turn to admire him. In fact, all she could think of was how rarely she had been close to such a handsome man, his hair well trimmed, and clothes neatly pressed. He had to be one of the beautiful people who frequented the outdoor cafes in the Village that she passed by unnoticed on her walks.

"Are you here to tour the property?"

Her warm smile revealed dimples in her cheeks. "No. I am here to do some local history research."

"Sounds impressive."

"Not so impressive as you may think but I am really looking forward to it. I assume you are here for the property aspect?"

"Yes. I am an investment advisor and checking this out for some of my clients. I have been looking forward to just getting out of the city for a spell."

"New York City?"

"Is there any other city?"

She laughed, realizing that she had not laughed in a really long time. Even had it been longer talking with a charming man. *But why is he talking to me?* "That is my home base too. I was anxious to leave for a bit."

"Ah, two city slickers lost in the sticks."

"Might be a good time for us to gather sticks."

"You are right about that. Are you an historian?"

"No. I have a passing interest in it. Actually, I am a writer."

"Non-fiction?"

"No, fiction is my forte. I have had three novels published."

"Wow. Now that is an accomplishment to be proud of. What is your full name?"

"Colleen McKenzie. Ever hear of me?"

"Sorry, I haven't. When I get back to a bookstore I am going to buy all three, I promise."

"Don't feel you have to do that. But if after you think about it you are truly interested, instead of developing an obligation with a perfect stranger, I have copies in my car. An author rarely is apart from her babies."

"Are they your only babies?"

"Getting a bit personal, aren't you? I have no children, no husband, and I do not even own a car. I rented this one to get here. I was surprised I even remembered how to drive."

"I'm not married either. I just have never met a woman that I desired to be fastened on to." The instant appeal of this woman, obviously devoid of the glamour and sophistication that he thought he yearned for, was as refreshing as the country air that filled his nostrils. "Maybe, this is the start of a beautiful friendship. I do want to buy your books."

"Or, the start of a character development for a future book."

"I am a character for sure. You need to interview me to learn the particulars. Will you join me for supper at the diner?"

"I'll think about it while I check in."

They entered the office and completed the paperwork. Colleen knew immediately why her aunt was attracted to the motel owner. His booming voice contrasted with a calm mannerism, and he was as friendly and talkative as she imagined an outgoing country man would be. Abner also liked her right away, recognizing the same intent eyes and genuine demeanor as Christine.

Grady and Colleen wound up in adjacent rooms, and there was even an adjoining door between the two rooms. As soon as Colleen entered her room, she slumped into the one armchair. *What would my heroine do now?* In a few minutes she knocked on the adjoining door. He unlocked it, and she said softly, "I will be pleased to have supper with you."

As Nathan Hoag neared the town of Bent Tree, the trip seemed shorter than when he had come with his parents for those summers at *Terra Firma.* Even though he was quite young then, he remembered those two summers as happy ones for the family. The disappearance of the fishermen had scared him and depressed his parents, but over the years the happy times took precedence in his mind. That is why when he saw the offering of

Paradise Gardens and figured that it was at the same spot as *Terra Firma,* he felt compelled to come here. He had retired as a teacher a year ago, earlier than he might have if his wife had not died of cancer. They did not have a perfect marriage, but the absence of children made their dependence on each other strong. After she was gone, a constant state of aloneness left him sad and distant from relatives and friends. It had gotten to the point where he convinced himself that he wanted to be alone as a form of penance. Maybe being in a place that once represented joyful closeness might help him to regain a semblance of peace.

He did not even notice the poor condition of the Skybridge Motel. He had become oblivious to even the most obvious things. In the office, a woman in an apron greeted him. Her hair was matted down from perspiration, and her bare arms revealed parched skin over firm muscles. No doubt a woman engaged in demanding labor.

"Hey there," she greeted him in a high voice. "I am Becky, chief cook and bottle washer. My father, Abe, would sign you in but he had to run into town for some essentials. Let me guess, you are the Canadian schoolteacher. Your glasses and stern look give you away."

"Am I that obvious? This is actually a disguise. I am the health inspector."

"Can't be. Never had one of them here, and if one ever did show up I'd tar and feather him."

"Then I better confess that you guessed right the first time. Of course, you have no way of knowing that at one time I was anything but stern. Sternness comes from seeing too much and understanding too little of it."

Becky smiled. "You're a schoolteacher alright. My teachers, as I can recall that far back, all talked in riddles too."

It was his turn to smile. "I bet you were a really good pupil. Probably too sassy for your own good but smart as a whip."

"Ah, you're a shrink as well."

"Just a passing observation."

74

"Is your wife here with you?"

He hesitated for a moment. "No, she passed away a couple of years ago. I was here as a child with my family and thought it would be diverting to be away from home and to catch a glimpse of an earlier period of my life. Being retired, I have more time than sense."

She sure did not understand all he said, yet she liked his looks, especially those riveting blue eyes behind the glasses. The balding head and slight paunch seemed to fit his overall being. If she had to describe it, she would call him cute and loveable. It was pleasant to listen to his soothing voice, and she bet he had been a wonderful teacher.

Nathan signed in and went to his room. He lay on the bed unaware that the room was quite clean compared to its ancient appearance. He could not get the image of Becky out of his mind, the first woman he had been attracted to in such a long time. Far from beautiful, she radiated a glow that could inspire poetry. Suppertime was suddenly a promising event.

Shortly after Abner returned, Gail Cohen checked in. He had not expected such a young person, although he had to presume that the Attorney General's office knew what they were doing. Somebody had to know what they were doing because he certainly didn't. They exchanged a few pleasantries, Abe figuring either he would find out specifically what she was after or if the opportunity arose in his innate forward manner he would just ask her outright.

The Lancaster boys were the next ones to arrive. They were anxious to find out which of their prospects had already been added to the guest list. Abner could not resist telling them that a lady from the Fraud Division of the Attorney General's Office had just checked in. Frank looked at Harold and shrugged his shoulders. "There's nothing going on to warrant any check on us. Sounds like a waste of time and energy, not to mention taxpayer money."

It was close to suppertime when the Pruitts arrived. Glenda looked spectacular. He had almost forgotten what a magnificent woman she was, and while he had no experience in the fashion world he just knew she was

75

decked out to the hilt. Everything she wore matched, and her hair was neatly in place. Gleaming white teeth matched the twinkle in her eye as she gazed at him. He took a deep breath knowing full well that his mind was comparing Christine to this magnificent female specimen. The difference was not disturbing. Rather it just confirmed that Christine was more to his way of life and thinking.

Glenda came back to the office ten minutes after they checked in. She moved close to Abner. "I came for more towels and what else you can give me."

Only his honesty, the very root of the integrity that composed his being overrode his male ego and inclination. The truth may not sound pretty but it has depth. "Towels, yes. Anything else, I can't. I am not good at explainin' things, but please hear me out. For years I had no one. Then, you came along and you are one spectacular woman. I am only human. You caught my fancy, and you're the first gal I have kissed in many moons. When it rains, it pours. After that, I met someone else who without the slightest effort captured my heart. Please understand, I think you're great. Maybe I should have my head examined. We are too very different people. Who we are and what would satisfy us beyond the here and now is not the same. Do you understand what I am sayin'? Do I make any sense?"

Glenda smiled and patted his arm. "I understand what you are saying more than you know, dear Abe. I came for a kiss and maybe more, and I received a slap in the face. It is what I truly needed and deserve. I am love starved, and reached out to you as a symbol, a form of salvation. It would have been a romantic fling for me, nothing beyond that. Maybe, it was just to prove to myself that I am still young enough to attract a man. In the end it would not have been fair to you or to me. I am truly happy that you have met someone who can be more to you than I could be. I will always dream of what might have been, no matter how temporarily." She stepped backwards, and he was not quite sure if it was a tear at the corner of her eye. "In the meantime, I'll settle for some towels."

He hugged her. "You are quite a woman. No wonder you are

76

successful. You have it all. I hope I can be half the person you are."

The construction crew had left for the day and Jack was double-checking to make sure everything was secure before he headed out. He spun around hearing a thud behind him. There lay a small dead bird. It must have fallen from the sky. He picked it up with a plastic bag and carried it to a clump of trees just beyond the excavation. As he walked back, he thought it odd that he had not seen any birds all the time he was there. Now, one fell dead some ten yards from him. *I do not like this. I do not like any of this.*

THIRTEEN

By the time Frank and Harold Lancaster arrived at the diner, there was a considerable crowd there for a small establishment. Nearly all the tables were occupied. Abner, who was waiting on the tables, came to greet them and started introducing them around. First, there was Mr. & Mrs. Murrow, then Mr. Reighton who was joined by Miss McKenzie, followed by Mr. Hoag who was sitting at the table closest to the kitchen, and then Mr. & Mrs. Pruitt who Frank already knew. He could not resist introducing them to Miss Cohen who was munching on a small salad, an open notebook lying close by. A few town folks were also partaking of Becky's luscious chicken stew.

The few times Becky emerged from the kitchen, Dwight tried to catch her eye but she was so engrossed in feeding the crowd that she did not even look his way. There was no other choice but to enjoy the delicious food and listen to Glenda who was more conversant than usual. It dawned on him that he had not really listened to her for a long time. He wondered just how long it had been that they had been taking each other for granted. As beneficial as it might be to take a respite during one's demanding drive for success, it can also be eye-opening as it affords the opportunity to calculate what has been overlooked along the way.

Frank and Harold just nibbled at the food as they were anxious to visit the tables of their prospects to give them a pep talk for tomorrow's visit to the construction site. They wanted to make sure the tour would be looked forward to as a prelude to snaring their prey.

Grady and Colleen would certainly find any intrusion on their

79

conversation a bother. Grady could not recall conversing with a woman that was this enjoyable. For Colleen, the freshness of it all was totally absorbing. It was an intimate experience she had not had before even if descriptions in her books had bordered on such a meaningful event. It was far more thrilling than she could have conveyed in a story line. The food loosened their tongues and they talked on and on completely oblivious to the others in the room.

That animated conversation was of special interest to Gail sitting at a nearby table. *Why can't I meet a man like that?* She tried to stay focused on observations of the Lancasters as they flitted around the room yet her mind kept wandering. How very easy it is to shift attention from what one has to what one is missing. A secret desire to be in Colleen's place took firm hold on her sights. There had been a couple of mediocre boyfriends in college and even a couple of her classmates in law school seemed interested in developing a romantic attachment, but she sensed that her intelligence and drive intimidated them to avoid overt action. She hated to think that the recipe of life provides that to get what you want you have to give up other things.

From his vantage point close to the kitchen, Nathan could see Becky through the crack in the door. She was the epitome of efficiency. There was a grace and dignity in the simple movements from the operation of the cooking to preparing the plates to be served. His eyes were riveted on this exceptional woman. Just when he thought he could never feel any emotion again, he reveled in the surprise to his mind and heart.

As the diners gradually left, only Grady, Colleen and Nathan remained. Abner went back to the kitchen and patted Becky gently on the back. "Well, little gal, you pulled it off."

"Not without the able assistance of super waiter."

"Glad to help. Real interestin' bunch of folks. Only the lovebirds and the Canadian teacher are left. He looks goofy-eyed at you. You sure have great power over men."

"Comes as a real shocker to me. He's rather cute and fascinating to listen to."

"A bit old, don't you think?"

"Since I'm no spring chicken, I'm not about to write anyone off."

"Since you say so. I'm with you lass, whatever. Let me finish up here and you go sit with him."

"I'm almost done, pop, thanks. I'll go out just as soon as things sit right ways here. Not sure I gave Dwight the cold shoulder on purpose."

"I had to drop the Mrs. She is a good sport. Took it real well. I have my aim on Christine."

"Good for you, you ole coot."

When she completed her clean up and set the stage for what promised to be a marathon breakfast for a puny diner, she went out and sat at the table where Nathan was sipping coffee. Her sigh was a mixture of relief and anticipation.

"Glad you came to visit, Becky. I sure did enjoy the meal. This is the best coffee I have ever had too."

She wiped her perspiring forehead on the soiled apron. "I bet you never saw a worse lookin' cook."

"You would lose that bet. I don't see a cook. I don't see anything bad."

"Open your eyes real wide."

"I've," he gulped, as he knew he could not stop the words from coming out, "opened my heart. That's where I see you from."

"Flowery words, teacher man."

"There is real substance behind those words. You must believe that I mean all that I say."

"I hope so. You have pried the lid offa my heart as well. It's gonna be real fun getting' to know you, teacher man."

"For sure, chef lady."

Abe, on the way out, stopped at the table before Grady and Colleen. "If you're waitin' for more food, we plum run out."

Grady smiled. "Couldn't fit another bite in anyway. We are leaving.

Thanks for the nudge. I'm sure you want to close up."

"See ya' bright eyed and bushy tailed early tomorrow for breakfast. Becky's biscuits will melt in your mouth."

Grady and Colleen walked slowly back to their rooms. Colleen felt as if she was walking on air. If this was real love it sure will provide some powerful infusion into her books. Imagination is wonderful but it cannot match the three-dimensional aspects of reality. She wondered if Grady could guess that she was a virgin. Still doubting her own self-worth and wondering what a handsome and sophisticated man would want to spend time with a bump on a log, she decided for the good of her writing she would ride this adventure through. When he kissed her at the door to her room it was a gentle, sweet kiss. "I'll knock on the door at 7:00 so we can have breakfast together," he said in a whisper. All that she could do was nod. It sure can be an earth shaking phenomena when a writer is at a loss for words.

FOURTEEN

The weather prediction was for a warm and sunny day. Before the sun rose, a dense fog hung over the lake. No one was around to see it. Not a soul to wonder why the fog swirled around slowly as if it had been stirred. When the sun peeked over the horizon, the fog disappeared as if a giant broom had swept it away. There was nobody there to see that either. Even if seen, it might have been difficult to believe. It might have been even more difficult to understand.

Dwight was the first person in the diner. He went back to the kitchen where Becky was stirring the batter for hot cakes. He grabbed her around the waist and tried to kiss her. She turned her head so that his lips merely grazed her cheek and then broke away from his grasp. "Oh," he said dismayed, "this is a cool reception for one who adores you."

She snickered, placing the bowl down on the side arm to the stove. "One who adores takin' advantage of an innocent country gal."

"No way. Do you think I am not earnest?"

"I don't know, poor man. You seem starved for affection, but I only feed bellies."

"Please don't belittle my attempt to win you over."

"I'm flattered, city fella, but there is just too much distance between us. You are a hunk, no question about that. You'd be a catch for a simpleton like me. But, you're too hot for a mountain cook to handle. Frankly, I have thought about you a lot. I may be unworldly but I do know my limitations. I could never keep up with you. I can't even keep up with you right now."

"Aw, don't say those things. I am not taking advantage of you. I am genuinely taken by you."

"By the thought of me? An easy conquest?"

"No, definitely not. You are what I have been looking for my whole life."

"If that is true, you sure look low. It can't be city man. Let it go. Your wife is beautiful and sophisticated. You deserve her."

"You sure know how to hurt a guy."

"It's my favorite recipe. I jus' don't get a chance to use it much."

Dwight sulked and turned to leave. "I think you are making a mistake."

"Probably so. It's not the first and surely won't be the last. I have been waitin' all my life for what you represent, but we just don't fit."

He passed Abner who was just coming in the door. Abe could see the rejection on his face. *My daughter, the manslayer.* He filled a cup with coffee from the urn and entered the kitchen. He kissed Rebecca on the cheek, noting the beads of perspiration on her forehead. The air was filled with the sweet aroma of freshly baked biscuits. "Good mornin', little angel. I had to go through a trail of broken hearts to git back here."

"He'll survive. I did him a favor. He'll realize it soon enough."

"From a slow life, you and me are suddenly in the fast lane. I'm not sure we, I mean I, can handle it."

"We can and we will, ole timer. Jus' keep lookin' ahead and not back."

"Sounds like a plan to me. Everybody needs a plan even if jus' for things that go haywire. That way, you can jus' blame it on the plan. Can I help with anythin'?"

"It's all under control, pop. I'm amazed at my own achievements. Jus' go out, enjoy your cup of joe and wait for that army to arrive."

"O.k., little darlin'. Give a yell if you need an extra pair of hands."

"Right. Jus' let 'em know they can have scrambled eggs, hash browns, biscuits or flapjacks, or any or all of it. The griddle is hot and I'm ready for the attack."

"Go for the gold, honey," he muttered as he left the kitchen to sit at the counter.

Grady had been restless most of the night. He kept trying to analyze his feelings about Colleen as if it was a financial transaction. That, of course, was the wrong approach. Once he discarded that cold diagnosis, he just concluded that she was a breath of fresh air in his stale environment. It mattered not that she was unattractive in the physical sense. He had his fill of so-called beautiful women. There was a sameness about women who care more for their appearance than the values of feelings and togetherness. Just as this trip had released the pent-up frustrations with his current life, Colleen was the spark representing a new pattern of emotion and direction for him. No woman had ever managed to have that much influence on him.

He dressed and went for a walk while it was still dark outside. A short way off he found a bench and sat there watching the dawning. The sunrise was a symbol or an omen, and all he knew was that he felt very much alive and not the automaton that he had been as he limped through each day as a painful exercise of personal futility.

Colleen had knocked on the adjoining door to make sure Grady was awake. There was no response so she figured he was in the shower. She had slept well, her body was relaxed as her mind was soothed. Yet, when the knock came at the room door, a slight quiver of excitement transversed her body. When Grady gathered her in his arms and kissed her, the thrill escalated. Once again at a loss for words, she reached out to hold his hand as they strolled to the diner.

Nathan entered the empty diner. Becky emerged from the kitchen smiling broadly. "Good day, professor. Coffee, perchance?"

"Sure would be nice. I take it black. I thought about you all night."

"Good cooks have a way of sneakin' into your dreams." She drew the coffee from the urn and handed the cup to him.

Nathan clamped his hand around the warm cup. "It's not your cooking. I had a good chance to see myself coming alive. I have been among the walking dead since my wife passed away, maybe even before

85

that. Life is very fragile. The separation between life and death can be a matter of inches or seconds or degrees."

"I sure don't understand what you say but it is a kinda music to my ears."

"That proves it. Only the intended can hear my heart sing."

"I'll listen to your pearly words later. Let me git you some vittles before the mob comes in."

Nathan sat at the same table he was at the night before, affording him the same view through the crack in the kitchen door of Becky moving around. Before she came out with his breakfast, he had a moment to reflect on this strong attraction he had developed towards this woman. As much as he thought he had loved his wife, he had never sensed this sort of powerful surge of emotion, not even in the courting days. He could tell she was also interested in him, but it might not be at the same level. After all, she was much younger and might even have other suitors. He was somehow going to give himself time to get to know her better and let her find out what he was really like. The scintillating sensation gripping his heart needed to be explored.

Grady and Colleen arrived just before Frank and Harold. Shortly after that the Murrows came through the door. Abe barely kept up with the serving function even though Becky turned out the food in masterful style. Dwight and Glenda were the last to arrive, followed by a few of the locals. The place was a beehive of activity and the din from the profuse conversations even reached Becky in the kitchen. All she could do was to shake her head in disbelief.

Abe and Becky let out a collective sigh of relief as the crowd left the diner, each raving about the breakfast. Only Nathan remained, and Rebecca came out to join him with a coffee cup in hand. "I guess I'll finish what's left. Your cup is still full, I see."

"My cup runneth over."

"Are you sure you're not a preacher?"

He chuckled. "Surely not. But you certainly are what I might have prayed for if I was." He drank the contents of his cup. "I've got to go for the tour of the property, but maybe we can talk later."

"Fine with me, preacher man. I have a ton of cleanin' up to do, fix lunch for a few stragglers, and then prepare a feast for this famished crowd. I couldn't prepare box lunches, so they'll all be starved on the return. Good thing you all leave tomorrow."

Dwight, Glenda and Nathan went in Harold's vehicle. The Murrows went with Frank. Grady was also to go with Frank but it was decided that he would follow in his own car so he could take Colleen. Besides wanting to be together, Colleen thought it would be beneficial to see the site in person to get a feel for it before she began the research endeavor.

The construction crew was in full swing when the convoy entered the area. Above the loud noise, Frank and Harold led the group from place to place within the confines, alternating between praising the development and accentuating all of the positives. The prospects were rosy and there was little doubt in their minds that anyone seeing the place and weighing its bright future could hardly refrain from becoming a part of it. Blinded by dollar signs can distort even the most obvious.

The Murrows listened half-heartedly, eager to get back to their room at the motel. It was comfortable there and the food was so good they complemented each other on their stroke of fortune to have taken advantage of this freebie. A glimmer of guilt at their lack of genuine interest was short-lived.

The Pruitts were quite disappointed in the lack of progress since their last visit and coupled with the negative turn of events with the Kressky family there was a mutual sense that they needed to talk more about this undertaking. There was still time left on the sixty-day kick-out clause in the contract.

Nathan had only a faint recognition of the beauty of the place, and if it were not for the fancy thoughts of Becky he might have been downhearted. His intellect knew that one cannot recapture the warmth and solitude of a distant past. Yet, he would always have wondered if he had not seen the place for himself. Certain remembrances should only be tucked into the files of a memory bank, to pull loose and basked in by thoughts in quiet times.

Grady was the only one who looked at it all with a trained financial eye. His experience and professional instincts dictated a conclusion that the project was far too ambitious to become a viable investment reality. Even if ever completed, it would only be on a scaled down version and initial investors would be highly at risk for losing all or most of the early influx of money.

If it were not for the close comfort of Grady's presence, Colleen had an eerie premonition of the undertaking. The saving grace was the stark beauty of the place, but it was a haunting type of aesthetics. It was as if the place resented being tampered with. They both agreed that the beauty would be far better protected in its natural state. It would be wonderful if they could come back at a later time to find it just that way.

Perhaps as a reflection of inner gloom, the calm fairness of the day changed rapidly. A chilling western wind descended down the slopes of the mountains and threatening storm clouds amassed on the horizon. They all piled into the vehicles before the rains came. Even the workers left before the muddy terrain would halt their efforts. None of them were unhappy about a shortened workday. Apprehension intruded on each construction action. It was as if they were waiting for some evil force to show itself.

FIFTEEN

"I feel rather uncomfortable about all of this," Dwight said grumpily once inside the motel room.

Glenda lightly touched his arm. "I agree. I just don't want you to lose any of your dreams. We have so few of them."

He hugged her. "Maybe it is time to build new ones......together."

She smiled. "That sounds like the Dwight I used to know and love."

"I guess I didn't realize how much I love you until we got back here. We don't need this condo to make our lives complete or fresh."

"I realize that now too. It's still early in the afternoon. Let's pack up and leave now. We can be back in the city tonight."

"That's a really good idea. I'll let Frank know we have changed our minds and tell him our lawyer will be in touch about terminating the contract. I love it when you are impetuous."

Abner was not totally surprised when the Pruitts hastily checked out. After all, he and Rebecca had given them a double whammy. He did not know they were going to cancel out on the *Paradise Gardens* contract, but he was not taken aback by it when he found out later. He knew he would miss seeing Glenda since she was a sight to behold for a mountain man. Classy women are few and far between in his meager existence.

Becky also was not shocked that they had left, although even in her simple country way she thought it would have been decent of Dwight to say goodbye. He could not have been as hurt as he pretended to be. When push came to shove, she was no prize package, and her sphere of influence barely stretched beyond the stove. As she dwelled upon it, she really did

89

not want to get away from here as much as she had previously wished. It is secure knowing one does what one is really good at, and she did not think she could ever tear herself away from her father. The mutual reliance was deeply ingrained. It would be a problem if this became an issue with Nathan.

Frank and Harold suffered a further setback at dinner when they moved from table to table to get reactions to the tour and to reinforce the prospect of any commitments. The Murrows were quite blunt in describing a lack of further interest. Grady was diplomatic in describing that some doubts existed that demanded further study before he could recommend any of this to his clients. Nathan portrayed a lack of enthusiasm while indicating that he might not totally foreclose the possibility.

"We have already had some disappointments here, Harold, but we will not let this sway us off course." Frank spoke in a near whisper to his brother at their table as they finished the pot roast.

"Let's be philosophical, brother," Harold responded in a hushed tone. "There are lots of fish in the sea. It's just that we are going to have to be super creative when we explain to the money people back home that this is taking longer to get off the ground than was anticipated."

"We're good at that, Harold," Frank said with a low laugh. "God knows we have had plenty of practice."

Gail Cohen took all of this in from her table in a corner of the room. The open notebook before her was filled with scribbled notes. She had purposely skipped breakfast and had gone early to the diner for lunch so she could question Becky. Becky told her what she knew, which was really very little and sketchy, and referred her to Abe.

After lunch, Gail went to the office and found Abe with his feet up on the desk reading a garden magazine. She spoke with him for about an hour. He was not specific, either on purpose or because he did not know the details, but was able to give her some factors she might consider in looking at the total picture. He was not reticent about exclaiming that he did not trust the Lancaster brothers. So, she planned to drive out and visit the site the following day after the tour crowd left. It would be Sunday, and she figured the construction people would not be there so she could look around unrestrained. That should wind up her work here, and she could return to Albany to work on her report.

At the University, Christine first received a telephone call from Colleen filling her in more about Grady than her research. She was truly happy that her niece might have stumbled into a romantic situation. Even an extreme introvert deserves that sort of exciting involvement. Later, when she talked to Abe, she jokingly suggested that he rename the motel *The Love Palace*. Abe laughed and proclaimed that it was all her fault for supplying the spark that had ignited all of the blazes. He told her he would take Colleen over to Mrs. Peabody's house on Monday. Christine was planning to come there on Thursday and stay for the weekend. That way she could check on Colleen's progress and be with him. That was all he needed to hear.

After the supper, Grady and Colleen walked over and sat on the bench that he had viewed the sunrise from. The rain had stopped hours earlier and stars twinkled in a clear sky. He dried off the remaining water from the bench before they sat. They kissed. Grady spoke first. "I hate to leave tomorrow but I have a full plate at the office on Monday."

"I understand. It will be lonely here without you."

"No. I don't think you do. Finding you has been special for me. I don't want to let it go."

She smiled and grasped his hand. "You don't have to. I will be back in the city by next weekend. My aunt is coming here on Thursday and, hopefully, by Friday I will have finished the research. You can see me there any time you want to. I warn you, I live in a hole in the wall." She was thinking to herself that once back to the reality of the city, surrounded by the women she could never be, he would quickly forget about her. Even if he tried to pursue a relationship, the economic differences would soon dampen his interest. A negative attitude is a tough shell to crack.

As if he read her thoughts, he spoke softly. "That makes no difference to me. Riches are inside people, and I suspect, no, I know, you are a treasure."

She looked deeply into his clear eyes. "I am naïve, poor, and a virgin. I have no experience with men or business. The irony of it all is that I write all about life in my books totally from my imagination. My contact with much I write about is nonexistent."

"A great resume, if you ask me, for someone I want to be close to."

"You're just being kind. What can you possibly see in me?"

"Try the world for starters. I also respect your virginity, and I would not want to violate any trust you might have in me until you are ready."

"Gallantly said. Just the right dialogue for a hero in my books. However, your patience might be truly tried."

"A challenge I readily accept."

They kissed passionately at her door. Colleen knew her books would never be the same again. Grady knew that the course of his life might not change but if he had his way he would not be going along alone any more.

Nathan waited for Rebecca to finish the cleaning chores in the kitchen. When she came out, he suggested they take a walk. They wound up on the same bench that Grady and Colleen had just vacated. Becky was the first to speak. "I'm awfully tired, professor. Go light on the lofty ideas as my pea brain can't handle much."

He smiled. "If you inspire me to great thoughts, who best to share them with? I do not detect a small brain in that lovely head. I do not think you give yourself enough credit. What I see is a competent person whose intellect dictates great achievements. Yet, I just wanted to tell you I can't say goodbye to you tomorrow. If it is agreeable, I would like to stay a few extra days, at my own expense, for us to get to know each other better."

"I would really like that. Things should quiet down after breakfast tomorrow and I will have more time and energy to try and absorb what you say, why you say it, and what puny comments I can offer."

"It will not be so burdensome, I promise. I am basically a simple person. It is just at times my ideas run into one another and talking about the consequences of the collision is not easy."

"I reckon that people are more important than ideas."

"I agree. It's just at times ideas can hold people together."

"If you say so. Walk me to the house. I need to flop into bed or I'll be a puny brain mess in the morning."

They walked slowly. He reached for her hand, and she wondered what his reaction was to her dry and rough skin. Working hands hold no secrets. He kissed her gently on the cheek at the door. When she closed it behind her, one weary thought seeped into her mind. *He's gonna be my man.*

SIXTEEN

They tried their hardest to be cordial at breakfast, and only their long experience in real estate capped the frustration. For Frank and Harold, who had counted on the initial purchasers to prompt a snowballing effect, even if it was only for the moment they were left empty-handed. Not only had the Pruitts left the fold, a couple of seemingly promising prospects slipped painfully through their fingers. It hurt the bottom line of the financial undertaking as well as bruising their inflated egos.

The Murrows quickly left after checking out and did not say a word to anyone. They did not even stay for the breakfast. Grady, after having the succulent breakfast with Colleen, thanked the Lancasters and diplomatically left the door open for any future contact. Nathan explained that he was staying on for a few days at his own expense and thanked the brothers for their hospitality. Gail was nowhere to be seen.

Grady led Colleen to the now famous bench, and it was his turn to be at a loss for words. How could he sound convincing to this woman that he had just met that his interest was sincere? This was not a financial transaction in which he would feel comfortable and polished. He had fallen in love with Colleen, a rather unique experience for him, but he knew she would look at such a pronouncement as suspect. It was going to be difficult leaving her, and even more of a hardship to leave the situation as resembling truth and believability. His thirst for a simple life, needing and enjoying goodness and warm closeness, was a shock to his being upon discovering that this was embodied in a woman. This had to be the most remarkable discovery of his life.

Colleen could tell that Grady was wrestling with himself, grappling for just the right words to tell her that this had been nice but this is where they part. He needed to get back to the reality that he was part of. She half expected to hear that sort of letdown. Yet, even in her limited experience with real people it struck her that Grady was a noble person. Even if he existed in a world dictated by the comings and goings of others and of commercial enterprises, there was a true person beneath any veneer that she was strongly attracted to. It was not just a gut feeling she had. There was an inner connection between them and a gravitational pull seeking closeness. She could not deny the strength of the emotion building in her mind and heart. Torn between wanting to clutch him and to hold on to him, and curious to know what she would feel once he left, in her writer's romantic predisposition she was sure she was in love. She would be a fool to blurt that out after such a brief time. He would think her reckless and immature. Would she actually be a bigger fool if she did not tell him and let him leave without revealing her innermost feeling? Her innocence and awkwardness, bordering on a cowardly fear of losing what she might not even have, left her mute. There was little doubt that her timidness left her wary of life and perhaps afraid of living the kind of life her heroines manage to garner.

So, neither one spoke any intimate thoughts. Rather, they kissed and he promised to telephone her when she arrived home. As he drove away, the thoughts were not on his business agenda but on a frail young woman with sad eyes and dimples when she smiled. It was a pure smile that melted his heart.

I will never see him again. Colleen watched the car disappear down the road. A new type of loneliness gripped her. She could successfully control the people in her books, an attribute that she did not possess for herself. Did the chance for happiness just leave her? Will she spend the rest of her life second-guessing? Will she forever doubt herself? All of this was fueled by a dismal thought. Her telephone number at home was unlisted, and he had not even asked her for that number.

Abner's directions led Gail easily to *Paradise Gardens*. She had figured

96

it right that there would be nobody else around on a Sunday and she could freely look everywhere. She was glad she wore her waterproofed boots. The area was muddy and the earth sloshed beneath her footsteps. It was obvious that there was an assortment of construction activity going on, but even to an untrained eye it appeared that more endeavors had been started than were being completed. It might very well impress one looking to invest that so much activity was in the works. Quantity does not necessarily equal quality. Another obvious conclusion that she jotted down in her notebook was that the site had no security. Materials and equipment lay scattered around unlocked and unattended. Nothing was covered either from prying eyes or the elements. Not a good way to run a railroad. Granted, the place was far off the beaten track. Yet, anyone with a truck and some muscle could easily enter and carry away a choice of machinery and equipment.

Gail could not deny that above the disorderly building activity, the place held a spellbinding beauty. The lake drew her as a magnate. She sat upon a log and gazed over the calm water. The liquid seemed unusually dark and a shudder passed through her frame. The eeriness led her mind to wander. Even though it was quiet, she did not hear or see the person moving swiftly and effortlessly behind her. Blackness, as of the water, obliterated her mind as she succumbed to unconsciousness.

When darkness fell, Abe felt uneasy that Gail had not returned. He entered the diner and asked Nathan to drive with him to the lake. On the trip, he filled the retired teacher in on the tales of mystery shrouding the lake, attempting to prepare him for any sort of dire discovery. Abner knew that evil was its own source of discomfort, and he could not recall any good ever coming out about the lake. Would this be just one more calamitous incident to confirm the savage nature of the water?

They first came upon Gail's car and the headlights of the truck did not reveal anyone sitting in it. Abner braced himself for the realization of the worst of his fears. They pulled besides the car, and Abe grabbed a flashlight from the bed of the truck and they started a systematic search of the grounds. The mud was up to their ankles. After covering the construction site itself and finding nothing, they turned towards the lake. The beam from the light caught the inert figure lying by a log near the water's edge. "Oh, my God," Abe stammered as he started to run towards the slumped over figure. Nathan joined him stride for stride.

In the stark light of the flashlight, Gail's face was pale, her lips had a green cast, and her clothes were damp from the descending dew. There was a pulse. He sent Nathan back to the truck to retrieve a blanket. They wrapped her in it snugly and carried her back to the truck. It would be a good forty-mile trip to the nearest hospital, so they decided to take her back to the motel first to see if they might revive her there. If they would be successful at that, Becky's wholesome soup would get her up and going. If they could not revive her they would have to summon an ambulance.

Becky and Colleen worked over Gail's form, and eventually her eyelids fluttered and she gradually became alert. With her bottom lip quivering, she looked at all of the concerned faces hovering over her and asked weakly, "How did I get here?"

There was a sigh of relief, nearly in unison. "You plum threw a scare into us, little lady," Abe exhorted. "You didn't return so Nathan and me went huntin' for ya. We found ya by the lake out cold."

She gazed from face to face. "Thank you. I sure don't remember anything. I was sitting on a log by the lake looking out over the water, my mind wandering I guess. I must have passed out."

"How do you feel now?" Colleen inquired.

Gail was slow to respond. "Not sure. I feel a bit dizzy and I guess shook up. I've never fainted before."

After downing some soup and hot tea, Gail went to her room to rest. Colleen helped her along. Just before she stepped into the hot shower, she felt a large crusty spot on her head through her hair. She parted the hair and gazed into the mirror. Above a bump there was an area of dried blood. Did she get that falling off the log? Did someone hit her on the head? Either way, she felt uneasy. There was a sharp sting as the water cascaded over the injury. Would she ever know what really happened? And, perhaps, even more crucial, why?

Nathan waited for Becky as the interested gathering dispersed. He knew she was very tired, but he did not want to waste a moment that he might give her a glimpse into who he is and his earnest interest in her. The conversation became more intimate as they walked along. Even through her tired eyes, she saw the knight on the white horse that she had always dreamed of. When they kissed good night, a warmth permeated the contact and a reassuring contentment rose and lingered. Who or how the personal history of two people falling in love is recorded is a personal matter that need never be answered as long as it is acknowledged.

The next morning, Gail and Colleen had breakfast together. Colleen had time before Abe was to take her to meet Mrs. Peabody. They lingered over the last couple of cups of coffee, and the conversation was lively and diverse. Quick friendships may also be the most enduring. For different reasons, neither had any close friends. Perhaps the paths through life were too arduous to afford the luxury of company. Both would come to analyze the new bond being created and come to the same conclusion. Close friends are one of life's distinct pleasures and should never be denied or rejected.

> *Friendship is a single soul, dwelling in two bodies.*
> Aristotle

> *The most beautiful discovery two friends make is that*
> *they can grow separately without growing apart.*
> Elizabeth Foley

> *A friend is someone who knows all about you*
> *but likes you anyway.*
> Anonymous

Before leaving with Abe, Colleen drove Gail back to the construction site so she could retrieve her car. Gail noticed that the crew had not yet shown up to work, and she thought that particularly odd for a beautiful Monday morning. In the distance she saw the log by the lake, and she just knew she would see that picture in her mind for a long time to come.

Gail and Colleen hugged before Gail started on her trip back to Albany. The mutual promises to stay in touch were not taken lightly. There are times in all of our lives when moments appear rather ordinary and mundane. Yet, in time they may gather great significance.

SEVENTEEN

"So, what do you think really happened to Gail?" Colleen looked over at Abe as he hunched over the steering wheel as they headed to Mrs. Peabody's house.

Abe kept his eyes straight ahead making sure the truck stayed a true course on the bumpy dirt road. He took a quick glance at the young woman in the passenger seat, her profile closely resembling Christine's, before he responded. "I don't think she fainted and fell off the log."

"She did tell me about the dried blood and bump on the top of her head."

"As far as I can figure, people don't get bumps on the top of the head from fallin' off logs."

"Do you think someone hit her on the head?"

"That'd be my guess."

"Who or why?"

"Hey, little lady, I'm no Sherlock Holmes. For me, just figurin' out how she got the bump is the limit of my detective ability."

"If you ask me, someone either has it in for the Lancasters or doesn't want the project to go on."

"Logical for an author. Maybe there's a book for you to write in all of this."

"Funny you should say that. I was thinking the same thing. Romances are fine, but I really think a mystery would be fun to write. I'm hyped up about it. There's enough intrigue here to fill up the pages."

"Go for it, gal. Your aunt would encourage it, I'm sure."

101

"Yes, she would. She is a wonderful person and very supportive."

"So I am findin' out."

"You really like her, don't you?"

"You might say that."

"I am happy for both of you. I should be so lucky."

"Why, lass, I thought you hit it off pretty good with that Grady fella."

Colleen sighed. "As a dream, maybe. I think I was just convenient and entertaining for him. He promised to call me when I got home. He didn't even ask me for my phone number."

"That's small potatoes, little lady. I forget details jus' from old age. A fella in love is gonna forget to put one foot in front of the other when walkin'."

"Do you think so?"

"I know so." Abe then thought to himself, *At least I hope I know so.*

Colleen smiled and felt relaxed. Abner was a really nice man and she wished her aunt would eventually marry him.

Audrey Peabody lived on a rundown farm close to town but at the end of some tricky roads. Her husband had passed away fourteen years ago, and she had attempted to keep the place running by herself. There had been no children, and the marriage had been more a matter of convenience than of love. Yet, she never had the nerve or means to break away. Over the long years of a barren marriage and beyond, her one real pleasure was in the collecting and maintaining the hundreds of books, files and papers dealing with the township. She considered herself the Bent Tree Librarian. She was proud and possessive of these holdings. The visitors were scarce, and it was a bright time for her to have one stop by to see the collection even if not perused. Not many people had a reason or desire to delve into this limited history. As she neared her eightieth birthday, being the keeper and preserver of the records was her compelling reason to keep on going. Without her, due to the lack of interest the collection would eventually be disbanded or destroyed. Her offer to turn them over to the main State

Library was politely rejected. Not that she blamed them, space even there was a problem and it would take time and personnel to catalogue the items.

When Abner telephoned her that he was bringing a researcher over to go through the collection, Audrey was thrilled. Old folks grab at straws for moments of pleasure and meaning. When the offering has a prebuilt handle to ease the taking hold of the person or event, the grasp can be especially important for the waning days. Even in her advanced years, she never stopped trying to figure things out, although not everything was clear or logical. One thing she did conclude about old people was that early and late memories are the most enduring. It was the mass in the middle that was blurred and disorganized.

Colleen's introduction to Mrs. Peabody was an added experience for her. She could not remember ever meeting or speaking with an elderly person. It accentuated the limited exposure she had to the world around her. The wrinkles in Mrs. Peabody's face and the stooped frame were clear evidence of a life of hardship, and she could not help but wonder if she was getting a glimpse of herself at a future time. Maybe young people should be more cognizant and understanding of the older generation. Feeling sorry for her, she had an immediate desire to draw close to the woman. Likewise, it had been far too long since Audrey had an occasion to converse with a young woman. She feasted on the happy face and just as Colleen had projected herself forward in time, Audrey recalled an earlier period in her life when her flesh immediately responded to instinct and her mind wasted no time in figuring out what was happening and what it meant. After the two were introduced, they chatted away.

Abner left Colleen at the farm and returned to the motel with the understanding that Colleen would call him to pick her up when she was ready to leave. If other days would be necessary for a visit, she would drive herself there.

Before showing her the books and materials, Audrey insisted that Colleen have a cup of tea with her. She served it in a cup yellow with age and accompanied by apple crisp warm from the oven.

"Well, dear, tell me about yourself," the older lady asked as they sat around the small kitchen table.

"Not much to tell, I'm afraid, Mrs. Peabody. I have lived a quiet and uneventful life. I am a writer and my books, depending on how you want to look at them, either tell the life I wished I had or the lives of others who have broken out into the world. I agreed to look into your collection to do some research as background on the lake for my aunt who is issuing a special report on the construction going on over there."

"Oh, that evil undertaking."

"Why do you say that?"

Her lack of experience with older people did not prepare her for the sequences, which would be repeated again, of a tendency to partially listen to what is said, even if the hearing was adequate, and to sway from the topic being discussed or the question being asked. "Call me Audrey, please. I know it is a sign of respect to address one older than yourself by their last name, but if we are to spend some time together I would feel more comfortable if you called me by my first name."

"Sure. I will be happy to do that, Audrey. Why do you describe the lake project in negative terms?"

"Even the younguns who come here call me Audrey. Some may feel insulted thataway. Not me. Makes me think they like me. It has been quite a spell since anyone has come. Carl Jenkins down the road drops off groceries for me once a week. Other than him, I don't get many visitors."

"I'm sure everyone likes you."

"Not so, child. There are some fearful forces in these parts, and there are them that hate me."

"I find that hard to believe."

"Believe it, child. Others get sucked into the quicksand. Some would have me dead and want my library destroyed."

"Why is that?"

"Some folks are good, some are bad. We have our fair share of the bad ones."

"Who are the bad ones?"

"The big apple tree in the back is even older than me. The apples just tumble to the ground. Good thing, too. I can't reach up to pick any. I used some for the crisp. Do you like it?"

"Yes, it is delicious, Audrey."

It became apparent to Colleen that she was not going to get any specifics. So, she let Audrey talk about an assortment of her personal agenda, and after she finished the tea she prompted the oldster to show her the collection.

It was all housed in a back room. It must have been a storage room as there were plenty of shelves along windowless walls. Colleen's guess was that Audrey canned fruits and vegetables when the farm was productive and the room held those items. The lighting was poor, and it took a few moments for her eyes to adjust to the dimness. Audrey outlined what was where, and she left Colleen alone to look around as she might care to do.

Colleen spent a few hours familiarizing herself with the contents of the room. Audrey had attempted to keep materials by age. That would be a help. When she felt she had a grasp on where she might start and proceed from there, she decided to come back all day on Tuesday and Wednesday to go through as much as she could to report to Aunt Christine when she arrived on Thursday. Until she started going through the material, it was unclear what she would find to help her aunt or what might be usable to her for any book she might write about the mystery of the lake. She looked forward to the undertaking, a mystery in and of itself. The one thing she reminded herself that was necessary was to bring along a lamp from her room.

She called Abe to pick her up. Audrey readily agreed to Colleen's schedule and offered to keep her fed with tea and apple crisp along with some other goodies. Company was a welcome respite to a lonely life. Colleen wondered if Grady would be disappointed if she got fat on apple crisp.

On the truck ride back to the motel, Abe told her that Grady had called twice. He would be working late at the office, and she should call him there. If it was really late, she should call him at home. Abe handed her a tattered piece of paper with both numbers scribbled on it.

Before going to the diner for supper, Colleen called Grady at his office. The number given must have been his private line because he was the one who answered. He blurted out how much he thought about her and how much he missed her already. He asked her for her home telephone number. He explained that in all of the excitement, he had overlooked that important detail. Then, in a serious tone, he indicated that her effect on him was deeply emotional and enduring. He exclaimed in an uplifted voice that he was in love with her. Of this, he was sure. Tears of wonderment and joy slid down her cheeks. Words would not betray her now. Her powerful response was as short and as sweet as she wanted it to be. "I love you, too."

EIGHTEEN

Over the course of the next two days, Colleen discovered some interesting information. During the teas and lunches with Audrey, taking advantage of her lucid moments as they arose, Audrey did answer some probing questions that tied together many of the cold and disassociated findings in the documents.

A small but important part of the collection was Indian documents from the Seneca Tribe, particularly the Tonawanda Indians. Most of these papers, on some sort of parchment, were written in the native language. Apparently, the elders of the tribe who were the only ones who could read that language had all passed away. The descendants had given up any interest in their contents. As a matter of principle, the elders had demanded on several occasions that Audrey turn that part of the collection over to them. Audrey repeatedly refused to do so, arguing that they were an integral part of the local history and to surrender them would be a blow to the integrity of the collection. When the conversant elders were still living and Audrey's husband was alive and fully engaged in running the farm, certain hostile acts had been directed at the Peabodys due to the refusal to give up the materials. Two of their dogs, at separate times, had been killed under suspicious circumstances. An occasional cow would disappear, and some crops were maliciously destroyed. There was never any definite proof who the perpetrators were, but there were no further incidents once the last elder died.

The bulk of the materials dealt with the settlers of the area and the growth of the town. Most of the influx of families to the area was as a

107

result of the promise of jobs to work on the WPA project for the roads around the lake during the Great Depression. The arduous project lasted years, and a good portion of the families just stayed on, settling primarily on farms. These folks engaged in agricultural pursuits just to survive, mostly in dairy farming. Some did start small business in the town, but the town never did prosper, and only a handful of those early businesses are still around. The area was always poor or slightly above the poverty level. Interestingly, the town never had a hotel or a restaurant. The Skybridge Motel and Diner had found its own little niche.

There had been great dissatisfaction with the road project. The workers did not feel adequately compensated for the type and extent of the work involved. The weather was often unpleasant and at times intolerable. There was insufficient clothing, food and housing for the workers and their families. Most of the shacks thrown up to hold the families had no good heat source and no indoor plumbing. The community well contained sulphur, fostering a foul smell and taste. The lake itself further contributed to the general aura of discontent. A brooding darkness of the water did not lift spirits as families derived little recreational value because the water was always too cold for bathing or swimming. Strange fogs and winds would come and go, and this added uneasiness to the place. Incidents were reported and documented that seemed to have no logical explanation for their causation, such as injuries to people and malfunctioning of equipment.

Despite the lack of benefits for all of the years, the people bound together in their common struggles and the community was strongly religious. The local church was packed every Sunday. Before busing began to the adjoining county schools, the children of all ages crammed into the inadequate schoolhouse. Colleen was surprised to discover that Audrey had been the school marm even though still a teenager. She had a gift, as described in many of the papers, for holding the attention of the children and was termed the smartest person around. Thus, over time it was natural that whatever papers or books the people had, they turned them over to Audrey. The library was created.

Gail's telephone call to Colleen on Wednesday evening rounded out the picture. Her discussions with a couple of staff members of the Attorney General's Office in Florida revealed some incisive glimpses into the antics of the Lancaster brothers. It brought a personal touch to the incidents covered in the file she had studied. They had been involved in a number of shady development schemes there. Because of scant concrete evidence, they had escaped any criminal prosecutions. Investors who had lost large sums of money had been unsuccessful in recovering damages in civil suits. The vagaries of the Florida real estate market and business developments in general had ended such attempts for recovery and left the brothers exonerated on each legal effort. As an aside, Gail indicated that she went to her own doctor about her head injury. The doctor was of the opinion that it looked like an injury caused by a blow to the head by a blunt instrument. The position of the injury on top of the head made it highly unlikely that falling off the log caused it. Sleuth Abe had been right on that analysis. Fortunately, an x-ray revealed no internal damage.

After hanging up with Gail, Colleen outlined her findings that she would present to Aunt Christine upon her arrival the next day. These would probably be the same threads of suspicious conduct to be employed in her forthcoming writing of the mystery.

Over the years, strange and perhaps natural occurrences connected to the lake and activities undertaken there have raised a boundless fear of the unknown. Such have been prompted and/or exacerbated by two malcontent groups. First, the Indians who, based on their customs, believed they have perpetual rights to the lake and its surrounding lands. The lake contains bodies and artifacts of the tribal history and is considered sacred. Any disturbance would be considered a flagrant violation of Indian rights. The WPA road project, Terra Firma (the cottage colony), and Paradise Gardens have been unwarranted intrusions on the spirits resting there and to the sanctity of the location. Second, the WPA workers and their families, past and present, feel they were abused by the system and never rightfully compensated for what they did and what they had to endure. An underlying grudge had developed into a vendetta over the years with the intent and design to assure that no other undertaking there should succeed where their exerted blood and sweat saturated the earth.

Most recently, a third group has entered the scene. These would be the people who suffered financial setbacks in Florida due to the alleged deceptive practices of the Lancasters and who, either in person or through agents, believe that these men do not deserve to prosper anywhere at any time.

Thus, any or all of these groups may have participated in some shape or form in the mysterious happenings of Tomb Lake. Which ones, and to what degree, will probably never be known. They are hidden in the darkness to match the blackness of the waters of the lake. It is unlikely that any further incidents will occur if the lake is left at peace. The tortured history of the beautiful lake and its surroundings seem to indicate that such serenity is well deserved.

NINETEEN

Christine was glad Colleen got through to her on the telephone before she left on the trip. The shaky news about the Lancasters that Gail had conveyed certainly raised a red flag for Christine. If there was a chance that she might not get any money from the slick brothers, she had better use some coercion now while she still had some leverage.

She called in Ann, her assistant, and dictated a letter to be sent to Frank Lancaster by courier. Basically, it indicated that by virtue of financial problems she would be unable to issue the final report on the lake project unless she received $8,500 to cover actual expenses to date and $10,000 for the final report. Instead of waiting for the full payment which by then could well add up to the $50,000 agreed on, she would accept the immediate payment of $18,500 as full compensation. From what Colleen intimated about the Lancasters, they would jump at the chance to save $31,500. For Christine, a bird in the hand in this instance would certainly be worth two in the bush. The money would still be adequate for her to leave academia and not only paint but also start a new life with the man she had fallen in love with. She was that sure of Abner. She was that certain about her own feelings and dreams. Too many people put off their personal rewards believing as a sure thing there would be little harm in a delay. Yet, so many vagaries of life and people can upset even the best-intended plans and most fortified of desires. Believing that this was her golden opportunity, she was not going to risk losing it by hesitation or postponement any longer than absolutely necessary.

Abe was outside mulching the plants for the onslaught of freezing

111

weather not too far off. He was dirty and sweaty when Christine pulled up in her car. With the bounce of a young girl, she sprang from the car and into his arms.

He could not contain the force of his embrace. "I'm filthy and sweaty, but it sure is good to hold you."

She smiled broadly, returning the power of his embrace. "I already know you are a dirty old man. Just the kind I like."

"Don't bother checkin' in. You're stayin' with me at the house. It's open. If you need help unloadin' or settlin' in I'll be finished here pronto. I'll clean up and give ya a hand."

"I'm not putting Becky out am I?"

"While you're here, she'll be stayin' with Nathan in his room."

"Oh, the Canadian Casanova."

"He's been stayin' on to woo Becky, and it has sure worked. She's fallen for him, poor fella."

"Do you think she'll go with him to Canada?"

"To meet his kin, maybe. I think it is more that Canada will be comin' to us."

"That's real good. I'm really only interested in you to get Becky's cooking."

"We already know that, don't we? All that sweet talk you pour out is false. But, lass, I'll take ya any way I can get ya."

Becky and Nathan grew closer each day. He hung around her every movement whispering words of adoration. She, in turn, encouraged him to talk about whatever might pop into his head. She was totally enthralled with his voice, the way he said things, and what he said even when she knew he was just babbling. Any impulse to reject him had long since flown the coop, and Becky was enjoying all of the attention.

They had numerous serious discussions since the night she came to his room to be with him. The lovemaking was gentle and completely pleasurable for her, and she did not mind coaxing his aging body to arousal. That she could do so was her gift to him. Their togetherness was sealed. It did not bother her that for the years they would be united she would probably be alone in her older years. Who knows, she might even die before him. Too many people think that life plays by certain rules. They do not apply for all. The vagaries of situations and accidental happenings, not to mention the health factor, can upset the smoothest of journeys. Yet, in the pretense of certainty and predictability, we think that it will all be as statistics prescribe. That projection can sag and break on the wings of reality. Such would be the advice she would offer to anyone venturing off the accepted and expected ways. It would be the pattern for her life quilt.

Colleen was still at Audrey's library, finishing the composite picture she would use as the background and travails of the projected book. She was making copious notes of factual instances to be incorporated into the story line. Tomorrow she would head back home and what promised to be a radically different life for her. The smallest of doubts and hesitation lurked about Grady's interest in her, but she was going to be as positive as she could be. After all, her future happiness depended on it. If that could be secured, the book would be the crowning achievement.

Colleen's reunion with her aunt was warm and the conversation flowed freely. Christine appreciated the research efforts and findings. The concise conclusions were just right for the final report, although she would probably leave out the part concerning enemies of the Lancasters. Christine would send her a check for time and effort as soon as she returned to the University.

Colleen was also uplifted by the animated romantic behavior of her aunt with Abe. *Can it ever be the same way with Grady?*

A heavy rain started falling, so at supper none of the locals showed up. Abe, Christine and Colleen sat at one table, and invited Nathan to join them. After she was sure all were served, Becky fixed a plate for herself and joined the group. Extra fixings were heaped in bowls on the table, and no one would leave hungry. It added to the joyous mood and all displayed high spirits. Nathan told a few jokes that kept the entire company rolling in laughter. Two sets of lovebirds and one love-stricken young woman can add a jovial touch to a feast and warm gathering.

Colleen was the first to leave, stopping by the office to call Grady to tell him she would start towards home tomorrow. He would wait for her call on her arrival and would then start down to see her. He could not put off being with her for one more day. Such an exclamation was thrilling for her, and she wondered if she was dreaming it all.

Abe and Christine left soon thereafter. They scampered through the rain to the house. In a matter of minutes they were lost in each other's arms, absorbed in the delights of the contact. These are truly enchanting moments worth waiting for. Both would agree it was long overdue for them and highly appreciated. They resolved to make the most of the precious moments they had together. Such can truly be referred to as the golden olden times.

Nathan kept Becky company in the kitchen and helped her when he could with the cleanup activities. "We make a good team," he boasted.

"I can see that. I do most of the work and you take most of the credit."

"Not so, dearest. All know you are the prime mover. I cannot and will not usurp your talents."

"You coat your words with syrup, that's for dang sure."

They conversed in detail about future plans. He would leave in a few days and come back for her just before winter's worst arrived. He wanted her to meet his relatives and friends. He would arrange to have his belongings put in storage, give up his apartment, and return with her to the motel. There they would stay together, get married and build a house for them to live in near the existing one. Fortunately, there was extensive acreage at the motel that Abe owned, more than enough to accommodate such a living arrangement. It would be their love nest. Nathan would gladly put his savings towards such an endeavor. His pension would carry them along even if the motel returned to its former debt laden ways. He would help her and Abe and would also take up music. He had played the violin when he was a boy, and although he enjoyed it the rush of life forced him to lay that aside. He had since then always had a keen interest in learning and playing a hammered dulcimer.

The plans discussed by Abe and Christine were not quite as firm. As much as she wanted to drop everything and come live with Abe and paint her way to ripe old age, there were just too many university commitments that would require her to finish the school year out. If she could get the money from the Lancasters, that should tide them over with the added comfort of her savings and small university pension that would kick in when she turned sixty-five. Weather permitting, she would come to him whenever she could. Thanksgiving, Christmas and the between semesters break would be the likely candidates if the roads were passable. They would marry in May when her duties were culminated, although their hearts and lives were already joined.

Long into the night, Christine awoke suddenly. Abe's deep breathing indicated a contented sleep. She lifted the arm that held her close to him and went to the window. Even in the darkness she could see the mountains against the starry sky as the rain had long since passed. She could not help but think of the lake. For all of the theories and interpretations of evilness attributed to it, in a way she felt drawn to it. Could it in some mysterious way have been instrumental in all of the love found and enjoyed at the *Skybridge Motel?* She shook her head knowing full well from her learning and experience that such could not be. However, it sure was a nice thought. This small group of people longed for and deserved some happiness. Wouldn't it be thrilling to pretend that a place of beauty, restless in that repose, while establishing a legend that all intruders who might infringe on that environmental majesty should suffer, could also engender love for all of those who respected that condition? The first painting to be undertaken would be of the lake. It would be her personal act of respect and appreciation.

TWENTY

Opening the door to her small Greenwich Village apartment, it still looked and felt cramped but the familiarity of her possessions and seeing things with fresh eyes, it was not oppressive. It also probably helped that the motel room was so small. This was her home and her workshop, and she did not sense the loneliness in the walls that depressed her when she returned from her walks. This was part of who she had been. It was not necessarily who she was going to be,

She called Grady, and he could hardly contain himself. He set out for the Village from his apartment up on Third Avenue. It took him about forty-five minutes to get there, and he considered it a lucky sign when he found a parking place right away.

When she opened the door, he gave her such a passionate kiss she could barely catch her breath. Once inside, he kissed her again but with a bit more moderation.

"Wow," she uttered, "have you been saving it all up?"

"I sure have. You are all I have thought about. You have cast some powerful magic spell on me, young lady. Have you gotten some supernatural ability from your association with the lake?"

"If it were only so. That might be a good angle for the book. I am all wound up about writing of the lake."

"And I am all wound up about you. The way I stayed close to you these long days is by reading all of your books. You write very well, and I hope you realize you are now living the ultimate romance on your own."

"A book could not fully capture the breadth and depth of what I

117

feel."

"I love you is a book in itself."

"I believe that now. Up to this moment, I still had a spark of doubt that you and what we have are real."

"Believe it, please. When I look into your eyes, I see today and all of our tomorrows."

"Corny, but I'll buy it. Looking back on it, I have many worse lines in my books."

"From heart to pen, and you can quote me on that."

She smiled and stroked his arm through the bulky sweater, "I have the sense that I am going to be using many of your quotes from now on."

Knowing she was tired, he stayed only about an hour. He would be over early in the morning, it being Saturday, and take her to breakfast and then to see his place.

An exhaustive sleep took her over. Yet, she could not recall when she was so at peace. Perhaps, that is the major proponent of love that gets overlooked because it is not dramatic or scintillating. It ushers in a calmness that makes all of life relaxing and enjoyable. Such a wonderful feature to bask in as it adds luster to each warm memorable moment.

Grady's apartment uptown had seven large rooms. Compared to her hovel, it seemed cavernous. With great pride, Grady showed her from room to room, hesitating on his books and records collections. He was especially intent on the paintings that adorned the walls throughout the apartment. One of his engrossing hobbies was to seek out budding artists not yet discovered where he could buy a painting that he liked for a reasonable sum. His particular favorites were watercolors of country snow scenes. Some had wonderful old houses or barns in them. A few of the houses were magically decorated for Christmas.

His coup de grace was an empty room at the back of the apartment that had an interesting view of the city through a large picture window. He held her close and boasted, "I spent several long nights cleaning this room out. It is to be your writing room after we are married and you live here

118

with me."

She was flabbergasted. "Is this a proposal?"

He kissed her gently. "Is it too mundane a way to do it?"

"How can any proposal from my love be too simple or too casual?"

"I am more certain of this than anything in my whole life."

"Then I certainly say yes. I love you a great deal. I can dream no better dream than spending my life with you."

"That dream will be as real as anything might be."

Before they actually set a date for the wedding, he took her to White Plains to have dinner with his family. His father was a retired banker and his mother had been a housewife all of her married life and had been active in charitable and civic organizations. Grady was the oldest child. There were two siblings who still lived at the house. One was a brother, Granger, now twenty-seven and an accountant. The other was a sister, Ginger, now twenty-four and a new pharmacist. The parents had been enamored by "G" names.

The family house was a large stone Victorian home on a large lot. It exuded an old world charm. The furnishings were beautiful, and Colleen had never seen so many antiques in one place.

The reception by and conversation with Granger and Ginger were friendly and entertaining. However, there was a noticeable coolness projected by the mother and father. Grady had not brought a woman home before to meet the family. The parents no doubt expected and were prepared to meet a more attractive and sophisticated woman, but they were cordial and Colleen anticipated that because of the evident mutual respect among the family members the parents would eventually warm up to and accept her as their son's bride, even if it was not whole-heartedly.

Unaccustomed to being in the limelight, Colleen had dreaded that meeting. It did not turn out as badly as she had feared, mainly because Grady kept her close and frequently espoused her virtues. His brother and sister's warm welcome also eased the way. When they left, Grady reassured her that all would be well.

In mid-October, a small wedding, with just a few friends other than family members, was held at the Reighton home. Aunt Christine came down from the University, Abe journeyed over from the motel, and Gail was delighted to be invited and drove down from Albany. Becky would have come as well but she was with Nathan in Canada. Abe just closed the motel for a couple of days since the diner was already closed. Christine and Abe huddled together content in the thought that their formal union would soon also become a reality.

The wedding dinner was catered at the home, and the excitement of the married couple buoyed the spirits of all in attendance. Colleen was particularly pleased by Granger's continuous presence by Gail's side, keeping her occupied in animated conversation. *Wouldn't that be an interesting development if it ripened into a romance!*

Colleen had already vacated her apartment and had moved her meager possessions to Grady's place, their love home. With the glee of a youngster, she had almost completely set up the writing room, having plenty of space to spare. It could, she thought, be a cozy nursery as well.

On the wedding night, at the apartment it was the first time they slept together. Grady was earnestly attentive in making love to her, emphasizing and slowly culminating each and every movement. He wanted the loss of her virginity to be a fulfilling act for her. It was that and more, and as Colleen clutched him to her breast she knew the full extent of love and happiness.

Grady had too many business commitments for them to take an immediate honeymoon. The next weekend he took Friday off, and they went to the *Skybridge Motel* for the honeymoon. Free room and meals were Abe and Becky's wedding gift to the couple. Abe beamed from ear to ear. In all of the long history of the motel, this was to be the first honeymoon spent there.

The timing was just right. Nathan and Becky had returned two days earlier from Canada. That trip had gone extremely well. Becky enjoyed getting away, and Nathan's relatives and friends were warm and fun. They were particularly appreciative that Nathan had met someone to ease the pain of the loss of his wife and that he would now have loving companionship. There was some regret that he would be leaving them, but the sad memories would also be left behind. Becky just had enough time to get fresh supplies, reopen the diner and get ready to royally feed the newlyweds.

That rundown place was where the two lovers had met and it would always be special for them. They also made two drives to the lake. The mired grounds from the apparent haphazard construction ruined the total picture but could not detract from the beauty of the lake. Both times they walked hand-in-hand down to the water's edge and sat upon the same log where Gail had received her injury. Both times, strange and wonderful occurrences accompanied their rest stop. The days had been chilly and windy, but as they approached the lake the wind died down and the sun seemed quite warm for a day late in October. The agitated water of the lake, driven by the winds, became calm and the surface took on a placid and inviting appearance. It was truly a time of peace shared by person and nature. Just as the motel was special to them, they also knew that this lake was always to be a significant element in their lives. The importance of symbolism embodied in all of the times of their togetherness was encased in the larger frame of this lake. It would continue to live in their hearts. It would endure forever in Colleen's book.

TWENTY-ONE

It was the week before Thanksgiving and the progress at the construction site was minimal. The work was far behind schedule. Jack Garland had an ongoing and agonizing feeling about the entire project. He had a nagging regret that as the construction foreman he bore the brunt of the grumbling from the workers below him and the impatient and demanding orders from the upper echelon.

On this particular day, as he drove his truck on the road along the lake towards the site, his troubled mind was in a state of high turmoil. The ground was already frozen, not all of the footers were in, and only one condominium section was partly erected. According to the master plan, it all was supposed to be under roof by now so that inside work could be done through the winter. It looked more and more now that they would be lucky to work up to Thanksgiving and he would then have to inform the Lancasters that all of the work would have to be suspended until spring. The recurring wish surfaced again that he hoped they would fire him.

As he drove along, he glanced sideways at the lake. There was a film of ice on the surface and, yes that is what it was, steam was rising from the ice giving the distinct impression that the lake was seething with anger. He hoped the men did not see it and start their eerie speculation about a breath of life coming from below.

As it turned out, fielding steam vapor suspicions would have been better than what the morning produced. Two heavy pieces of machinery failed to start. A cross beam fell from its lodged place in the one existing partial structure and injured two of the men. Rather than wait for an

123

ambulance to come the forty miles from the hospital, Jack was going to set them in the bed of his truck, cover them with blankets, and take them to the hospital. Just as he was starting to leave, one of the other workers had a heart attack and died before anybody could get to him. That did it. The rest of the crew headed home, leaving Jack at the site with the two injured workers and a dead body. There was no choice now; he had to send for an ambulance and wait for the authorities to arrive.

It was long into the night by the time he had filed the police report and left the hospital. Facing the grieving widow of a man far too young to have died and the families of the injured capped one miserable day. But, it was not the end of fast moving negative developments.

Arriving at the house, his wife, Mary, told him that Frank Lancaster had called and Jack was to telephone him the minute he got home no matter how late it was. As he dialed the number, he looked at Mary and realized how their difficult life had aged her prematurely. He had only to look in the mirror to know that it was his fate as well. He had not been able to give her a comfortable or secure life. They were always moving from job to job, whenever one would become available. Long periods where work was scarce and money short took a toll on their physical and emotional well being. They never had any children and while they did get along reasonably well, many more things were left unsaid than spoken.

Frank's news was not the icing on the cake, it was the blood on the floor. The plug was being pulled on the project. The money backers were withdrawing in part because of disenchantment with the lack of sales and in part because a deep recession was taking a stranglehold on the economy. Jack was to inform the workers and tell them they would receive their last paycheck in a couple of weeks by mail. Jack was to supervise at the site as the business equipment companies came to retrieve the rented machinery and a salvage company would take whatever materials were not already used. The site would then be abandoned as it was while the brothers put it on the market for an eventual sale. Frank hung up before Jack could brief him on the bad news of the long day.

As he sat down at the dining room table to pick at the warmed over supper, he told Mary of the deflating events of the day. Mary then went into the living room to watch television. She returned to the dining room when she heard him sobbing. His head was buried in his cupped hands. She put a weak arm around his shoulders and patted his arm. "Let it all out, dear. We have been through things like this before."

She was right. They had hit bottom a number of times. Yet, just when it had seemed darkest, a door would open and a crack of light would be let in. He was tired and frustrated but he refused to give up hope. Mary would see to that.

As he and Mary sat down for a minimal Thanksgiving dinner, the plans that had been forming in his mind were coming into clear focus. The seed of the smallest idea can come to bountiful fruition. He carved the small turkey, the bird seemingly having suffered a deprived life as well, and he smiled at Mary. She never gave up on him. She had to endure with so little, and not once did she complain or berate him about it. She knew Jack was a good man and firmly believed that goodness would enable them to survive. She returned his smile. After the meal he told her of the exciting plans he had come up with. No stranger to risk taking, this might prove to be the barest of chances for some success.

He was tired of moving around. This small rental house was comfortable for the two of them and the rent probably more reasonable than they might find elsewhere. While this town and county were poor and there was unlikely to be any construction activity, there was no business engaging in construction anywhere close by. They would stay in the house and he would start a fledgling construction/home improvement business. A few of the construction workers who were exceptional craftsmen and easy to get along with were eager to join his venture when he explained it to them. It would be taking a monumental chance and it would be a struggle, but it just might pan out. Mary was happy to see him involved with a dream, and she would surely stick with him no matter how long and hard the road might be. She would give him whatever support he might need, and suggested she could do whatever clerical duties were necessary. He looked at her with a great understanding and appreciation for the wonderful person she was. He hugged her, sensing the weakness in her limbs while exuding great strength of character. In spite of all of the setbacks, he was truly a lucky man.

The harvest materialized sooner than he could have imagined. Shortly after the new year began, Grady Reighton telephoned him. Abner had told him about Jack's going into business for himself. Grady and Colleen, after finding out that the Lancasters had put the lake and surrounding properties up for sale, bought it from them for the low price they had originally purchased it for. The Lancasters considered themselves fortunate to have at least recouped that money through a quick sale. They had braced themselves for a long haul and due to the shaky economy probably selling it all at a very depressed price. Now, Grady and Colleen wanted to hire Jack to work just as soon as the weather allowed to remove any vestige of construction scars, or at least to cover them up, and to restore the area to as close to a natural condition as possible. Jack was told the young couple wanted to preserve the area and had vowed not to let any construction activity to detract from the peaceful scenic place.

Shortly after receiving that job, Jack was contacted by Becky and Nathan. They wanted Jack to build them a house on the grounds of the motel just as soon as he finished the work for Grady and Colleen. They had developed plans for a log home. Mary was delighted with the prospects. It might very well turn out to be a successful year and a good life.

TWENTY-TWO

Christine could hardly believe that it was May already. The school year had ended, the faculty had held a farewell party for her, and she had managed to get all of her school belongings into the car. She hugged Ann after giving her an extremely complimentary letter of recommendation. The one remaining task for her able assistant to do was to meet the moving van at Christine's University housing unit so the contents could be loaded for the trip to the mountains.

Ann was thrilled by the letter of recommendation and was confident it would open many opportunities for her after graduation. She was so glad she had paid no heed to the stories of Christine's tyrannical behavior with assistants. She did not feel like her underling. Christine always treated her fairly and was always respectful. Ann was also most appreciative of the $2,000 check Christine gave her from the proceeds from the Lancasters. They only paid Christine $8,500 claiming they no longer required the final report. However, she was content to receive even that amount, as she feared not receiving anything under the circumstances of the terminated project and the devious character reputation the brothers had. She dreaded having to bring a lawsuit although she would have done that if it were necessary.

That final report, while unwritten, had festered in Christine's mind. While she tried to concentrate on the forthcoming double wedding of her union with Abe and Becky's hitch with Nathan, she had spent too many professional years in her field of expertise to dismiss matters that appeared to have no logical answer. Ever since the lab analysis returned negative findings on the water and soil samples, she was puzzled by the absence of

127

fish and other wildlife at Tomb Lake. Accustomed to resolving the smallest of details, unanswered questions were a supreme test of her intellect.

The timing of the double wedding turned out to be perfect. The civil ceremony was to be held behind the motel on the spot where the following week Jack and his crew were to break ground for the log home for Becky and Nathan. An unusually early spring in the Adirondacks had allowed Jack to start on the Tomb Lake job early and to finish it the week before the ceremony.

Grady and Colleen had come up a couple of days early for the wedding to check on Jack's work and to take a brief vacation. A heightened excitement took hold as they drove to the lake, their lake. They were once again struck by the majestic beauty of it all. It was breathtaking and satisfying to know it would always look like this. Jack had done a masterful job. The only sign that anything had disturbed the environment was the freshly turned over and fill-in soil. Over the ensuing years, vegetation would take it over and completely hide any scars. It would all be as it should have remained.

Colleen was four months pregnant, and Grady was overly protective as he was prone to be. A forthcoming grandchild had removed the last vestige of doubt of Colleen by Grady's parents. An added ingratiating sentiment was that the couple did not want to know the sex of the child before birth, and they would name him Gordon or her Grace, as the case may be. So, the "G" tradition would be ongoing.

Abe wanted to get a caterer for the reception so that Becky could fully enjoy her day in the sun. She would not hear of it, and prepared everything the night before. It was to be a small reception and the preparations did not overwhelm her. Besides the loving couples, only Colleen, Grady, a few long-standing local acquaintances and the Justice of the Peace were there. At the last minute, Jack and Mary were invited. A close friendship was budding, and they took particular joy in being there with the people who gave them a needed boost. A simple act of inclusion can produce a major sense of belonging.

A better day could not have been ordered. A warm sun enveloped the group touched only occasionally by a gentle breeze. The flowers that Abe had planted nearby had bloomed as an accompanying orchestra. Vows were exchanged and destinies formally interlocked. It was a magnificent day of love, long to be remembered and often to be celebrated. Including Colleen and Grady, six lonely people traveling along separate roads had met at a crossroads to discover only one road went from there. Together, they decided to venture forth wherever it might take them. Mary had espoused the right formula. For good and deserving people, a wonderful future beckons.

TWENTY-THREE

A week later, Christine set up her easel and canvas by the lake. She knew just the place she wanted to paint the alluring sight from. It was where Abe had first kissed her.

When she had mentioned to Colleen that she was going to paint a picture of the lake, Colleen was ecstatic. She was only about halfway through with the writing of her book, but she convinced her aunt to allow her to use that painting for the cover of the book. She termed it as not only appropriate but also as extremely meaningful. Christine was not sure that her as yet untested talent would match the needs of the proposal but she was flattered. It also served as an added incentive, as if she needed that extra drive. She had already decided that if it turned out fairly well and Colleen really liked it, she would give it to them. It would be a gift for them and the baby. It would be a significant addition to the paintings already on the walls of their home.

To her amazement, a fish jumped out of the water some one hundred yards away. A few small birds flew by and landed on a bough of a tree nearby. A hawk circled above the lake, perhaps attracted to the jumping fish. Off at the edge of the woods, a doe and her two fawns were grazing on emerging buds in the underbrush. A squirrel, holding on to the trunk of a tree, watched the feeding with keen interest.

The joy of the act of painting, and the pleasure in the subject of the art, led her over the ensuing days to ponder what it all means. In this kind of solitude the beauty of and the forces of nature meld. The lasting lesson to be learned is that while nature can exhibit a form of restlessness that may

131

well bring cruel and harsh results, it can also be a source of satisfaction and contentment that can usher in or foster good things. She had an urge to be a part of it. Tempted as she was to include herself in the painting as a small figure by the edge of the lake, she dismissed that notion as it might detract from the true insight of the painting.

Her now intimate association with the lake on a daily basis gave her the sense that this pastoral lake had been forced to play many roles. Its favorite had to be when it was resting. Colleen and Grady would see to it that this would be its permanent state. She hoped the painting captured that essence of tranquility. When the painting was finished she showed it to Abe for the first time. He exclaimed that he had never seen a painting that was so beautiful, and he once again knew how talented his wonderful wife was. His comment was followed by this telling remark, "The lake looks so peaceful."

Daniel Hill Zafren

www.ingramcontent.com/pod-product-compliance
Lightning Source LLC
Chambersburg PA
CBHW051846170626
46807CB00003B/1374